EMERGENCE
THE BELT

'I absolutely loved this... all action and brilliant characters..'

'I read a lot and every now and then there is a real gem. This is one.'

'An amazing story from start to the superb and thoughtful conclusion.'

'Wow. Couldn't put these books down. All so well written as one story led into the next.'

'The Belt series is probably the best new addition to the hard scifi genre that I have read in 20 years.'

'Awesome Read. Couldn't put it down. Exciting twists and turns.'

'Super story from a great writer! Great characters and plot lines. A great read!!!'

'Fast moving and entertaining, a real page turner.'

'If you enjoy science fiction that isn't about marauding aliens, you'll enjoy this series as much as I did.'

BY GERALD M. KILBY

MOON BASE DELTA
Solar Storm
Resource Control
Power Vacuum

THE BELT
Entanglement
Entropy
Evolution
Enigma
Exodus
Emergence

COLONY MARS
Colony One Mars
Colony Two Mars
Colony Three Mars
Jezero City
Surface Tension
Plains of Utopia

TECHNOTHRILLERS
Chain Reaction
Brain Gain

SHORT STORIES
Gizmo Origin
Winds of Mars

EMERGENCE

THE BELT : BOOK SIX

GERALD M. KILBY

OUTER PLANET
MEDIA

For notifications on upcoming books and access to my FREE starter library please join my Readers Group at geraldmkilby.com.

CONTENTS

1

THE DILLON WAYSTATION

The Dillon Waystation is as close as you can possibly get to nowhere in the asteroid belt and still order a drink. Its isolation suited people like Dakota Baird and his motley crew of privateers—along with a sizable contingent of like-minded individuals who preferred to play by their own rules, far from the prying eyes of civilized society.

With the QI on Ceres long gone, opportunities for the smugglers' trade had become plentiful. A little anarchy went a long way when your business was all about slipping under the radar, doing what needed to be done, no questions asked. At least that was until the Xiang Zu Corporation decided to start a war for control over the region's resources.

"Are you in, Dak?" Jarvis, one of his crew, gestured at the chips piled up in the center of the grubby bar table, which had been fashioned from an old airlock hatch. "Too rich for you?"

He cracked a smile, exposing a row of teeth reminiscent of a crater rim.

"Eh?" Dakota glanced at his cards. *Three kings, and all cards out—tricky*, he thought. There was already an ace face-up on the table. Could be very useful to someone, particularly if they happened to have a few more. He glanced around at the others, trying to divine some meaning from their body language. But all he could tell for sure was that they were mostly drunk.

"Okay, I'm feeling lucky tonight." He slid a stack of chips toward the ever-growing pot. "I'll see you and raise you twenty."

"Twenty?" Tamires was next. She tipped her head from side to side, weighing up her hand. Then let out a long sigh. "You know, maybe if we got paid from that last job I wouldn't have to gamble for my next beer." She threw in the last of her chips. "All in, I suppose."

"Say, boss." Brooker, one of the techs, looked over at Dakota. "How's that coming along? I mean, when do we get what we're owed from those Xiang Zu bastards? Been waiting a long time."

"Yeah," Aeon piped in. "We're all running on fumes. These recent jobs pay crap."

Dakota raised a hand. "Soon, very soon." He gave a quick scan around the bar, checking out the collection of patrons who had gathered here tonight. He recognized many of the usual crews, but some he did not. New people had been arriving of late, many of whom were just young radicals escaping the drudgery of Belt life for the prospect of danger and excitement. But there were others that had clearly not opted for this life by choice. They were here because they had simply nowhere else to go. Their old life in the Belt had been destroyed by the growing conflict. This was the only option they had left. But they would never survive; Dakota knew this. They just didn't have the temperament, the ruthlessness—they would all be dead within the year. In the meantime, the only person who would grow rich from all this new activity was the owner of this backwater establishment, Dillon Barr.

He had been a mercenary turned smuggler back in the day, long before the QIs started getting involved, and his past was the stuff of legend. How much was true and how much was myth really didn't matter. What mattered was that he was so successful that other crews began to rely on him to find jobs. But what really set him apart was that he could be trusted—possibly the most valuable asset in the Belt. But he was also a masterful strategist with a keen instinct for making a buck, and saw the writing on the wall when the QI on Ceres finally went live. He chose that time to get out of the business, deciding instead to put all his energy and resources into acquiring an old decommissioned ore-processing station that was ready to be junked. He towed out to the asshole of nowhere and got busy turning it into a waystation for the crews that operated all across this sector.

Most people thought he was crazy. But they were people that didn't really know him. They just assumed he had taken too many pills or too many plasma blasts to the head and had lost a few marbles in the process. Yet what Dillon knew was that the second-most precious thing in the Belt, after trust, was gravity. In a region where the biggest rock had barely 3% of Earth's gravity, the population out here spent most of their time and resources finding a place to hang out that had a decent level of artificial gravity. And the old ore-processing plant that he had just acquired had a gigantic rotating torus generating a full one gee.

So, over the years, Dillon set about turning it into a place where crews could hole up for a spell between jobs. Where they could fix their ships and equipment, replenish their supplies, and kick back for a time while they hunted down the next gig. Soon, as crews came and went, got drunk and started talking, Dillon Barr knew pretty much everything that was worth knowing in this sector of Belt space. All information flowed through Dillon—he was a clearing house of knowledge, and that proved to be worth more than even he ever imagined.

Dakota was damn sure that Dillon knew his crew were responsible for the takedown of that Mars ship a while back, and he might even know what it was they stole. That was dangerous information. There were quite a few crews in the waystation tonight who could get very upset if they were to find out what Dakota had stashed away in the cargo hold of his ship. Even more so if they knew that the client was none other than the Xiang Zu Corporation. The very people they regarded as responsible for their sudden change of career.

He turned back to the card game with his crew and leaned in over the table. "And keep it zipped." He jerked a finger at Brooker. "Don't say that name in here again. Not unless you want to fight your way out."

Brooker scowled. "Just saying. We've been sitting on this for months. It's time we got rid of it."

"Yeah," Jarvis whispered. "What's the big hold up, anyway?"

"I said, this is not the place." Dakota scowled. "Let's get back to the game. Aeon, you in?"

Aeon studied her cards.

Dakota glanced over at a dimly lit alcove where Dillon held court. He was nearly always there, sitting in the same place, engaging in whispered conversations with those in the business that mattered, while two heavies stood guard, fending off any losers desperately seeking Dillon's ear. He looked up at that very moment and caught Dakota's eye. He nodded, smiled, and raised a glass. Dakota nodded back an acknowledgment.

"Screw it, all-in." Aeon pushed the last remnants of her stash into the pot and slapped the table. "Time to show what you got, ladies. Dak, lay them out."

Dakota placed a king face-up on the table, followed by another, and after a short pause for effect, another king.

Jarvis let out a groan. "Goddamnit, I had three queens." He threw his cards down.

"Well, well, well, what have we got here." Aeon placed an ace down next to the one face-up on the table. Dakota knew what was coming. Then another. Three aces, he knew it. He should have folded when he had the chance. But Aeon wasn't finished; she rubbed salt in everyone's wounds by placing down another. "Ha-ha, four big ones, full engine burn. Aaaaand... that's mine." She reached across the pot with both arms and scooped it over to her.

"Jeez, Aeon. You're buying the beer from now on, you just cleaned me out." Tamires shook her head.

As if on cue, at the mere mention of the word beer, one of the staff approached their alcove. But before he took any orders, he moved over beside Dakota, bent down, and whispered in his ear, "Mr. Barr insists you join him for a drink."

Dakota glanced over, but Dillon was engrossed in conversation with two people who looked more like anxious refugees than hardened mercenaries. *Is Dillon going soft?* he wondered. "Sure." Dakota nodded.

Another round was ordered by Aeon, the waiter moved off, and all eyes around the table looked at Dakota.

"So?" said Jarvis.

"So"—he jerked his head over at Dillon's alcove—"the great man wants a word."

This was met with silence, interspersed with quick glances around the bar. Dakota, like his crew and everyone else within a million kilometers of this waystation, knew that Dillon was not someone who indulged in idle chat. When he invited you into his inner sanctum, it was because he wanted something, and it was never a good idea to refuse.

"Crap," said Tamires. "I bet he knows about the—" But she was cut off by an elbow in the ribs from Jarvis.

"Don't bloody say it, not in here."

"Well, only one way to find out." Dakota stood up. "Catch you later." He strode off to meet with Dillon Barr.

Dakota felt a strange vibe in the waystation as he threaded his way over to the seat of power. With this many patrons the bar would normally be borderline manic, but not so tonight. Most had gathered in tight knots of hushed conversations in dim corners. Nobody seemed in the mood to party.

Dillon glanced up as he approached and somehow sent a silent signal to the two heavies to let him through.

"Ah...Dakota Baird, good of you to join me." He gestured at a seat opposite.

Dillon was not alone. In fact, Dakota could never remember a time when he wasn't surrounded by a circle of minions and lackeys. Even now, there were several others skulking in the darker recess of Dillon's alcove.

Dakota sat, and cast a quick glance at the two people leaving. From their clothes and general body language, they didn't get what they came for. He jerked his head at them. "Taking on new staff? Business must be good."

Dillon gave a wry smile, and stroked his long red beard. "Ah...there's a lot of uncertainty these days, too much chaos going on in the Belt. They all hang around here, looking for a way out."

A waiter came with drinks; a beer for Dakota, water for Dillon. He took a sip and sat back. "Those two came with news from afar." He jerked a thumb over one shoulder. "Refugees from Eugina. Bad things happening out there." He waved a hand in the air. "But I'm sure a man with your connections knows all this, can smell the change in the wind."

Dakota took a long drink, more to steady his mind than to quench his thirst. He needed to be careful with Dillon. He could draw you in with seemingly trivial banter only to pounce once you let your guard down.

"A little anarchy has always been a friend to those in our line of work, Dillon."

"Ah...Dakota, ever the opportunist. A silver lining in every cloud, yes?"

Dakota nodded. "You could say that."

"Yet"—Dillon shifted in his seat and focused his steely green eyes on him—"what if that cloud is the harbinger of a great storm, what then?"

"Then it's best to find a safe harbor and wait it out."

"A wise choice." Dillon sat back, broke off his stare, and stroked his beard again. "Tell me," he said after a while, "do you know anything about a Mars ship that was rumbled a few months ago, over in the Eros sector?"

There it is, he thought. Dillon knew damn well it was his crew that did the job. *So, what's he after?*

"Ah...ships get knocked over all the time," Dakota replied with as much disinterest as he could feign. "So much so that the details can get a little muddy."

"Well let me help you. This one had a cargo of particular interest to the Xiang Zu Corporation."

"Oh?" Dakota examined the interior of his glass.

"Yes, and rumor has it they still haven't taken delivery of it yet." Dillon glanced around, leaned in, and lowered his voice. "They say it was a quantum core that was stolen. One destined for the New World One habitat." He leaned back again. "As you can imagine, that's got a lot of people interested as to the whereabouts of this cargo."

"Really? What sort of people?" Dakota took another drink to steady himself.

"Desperate people, Dakota." Dillon almost spat out the words. "The worst sort. Desperate people do desperate things."

He let this hang in the air for a moment, then jerked a thumb over his shoulder. "Take those two unfortunates that were here earlier. Lost everything back on Eugina. Everything they thought was important in life, poof! Gone." Dillon locked eyes with Dakota. "You see, they naively thought they could hold out against the Xiang Zu Corporation. Well, they were wrong. And now what they got?"

Dakota struggled to reply before Dillon spared him the misery by starting up again. "Well, I'll tell you what they got. A rumor is what. A rumor about a magical computer that can solve all of their problems." He held Dakota in his gaze for a moment, then shrugged and sat back. "Ah...maybe it's just bullshit, you know—a myth, a specter. But it's what gives them hope, keeps them going, drives them on. Desperate people, Dakota, they got nothing to lose."

Dakota sipped his beer and took a moment. "Well, that's fascinating, Dillon. You do have the best stories. Sorry I can't shed any more light on this...rumor."

Dillon nodded. "Pity." He took a sip of his drink. "Do you know where they're heading next?"

"Can't say I do, Dillon. Nor do I really care."

"Well, you should, because they're looking to buy passage to Elektra where they've vowed to hold out against Xiang Zu, come what may." He gave Dakota a considered look. "Isn't that where your brother and family are? Surely you must be worried for them?"

Dakota felt the blood pulse in his temple, and only for the fact that weapons were banned on the waystation, he might have blown Dillon's head off. "That's no concern of yours."

Dillon raised a thin hand. "My apologies if I've touched a raw nerve. Families can be so complicated." He smiled.

Dakota downed the last of his beer and went to stand up and leave. But Dillon raised a hand.

"Sit."

He felt rough hands grab his shoulders from behind and shove him back down in the seat. Dillon leaned in, his face deadly serious. "I know you did that job on the Mars transport. I also know that you're still holding the goods. I don't know where you have it stashed, but even if I did, rest assured, I want no part of it. Because it's a poisoned chalice, Dakota. Ready to bring hell down on anyone who has it."

Dakota said nothing. What was there to say?

"Now you and me, we go back a long way, back to the early days. And it's out of respect for you that I'll keep this our little secret. But I want you off this waystation, right now. Your crew have already been shown the door. They're waiting for you on your ship. I want you as far away from here as possible." He paused to let this sink in. "But as a parting gift, let me give you some advice. Like I said, a storm is coming, but this one has no safe harbors, it only has sides, Dakota. Best make sure you're on the right one when it breaks."

He nodded to his goons. "Get him the hell out of here."

2

LIFE GETS COMPLICATED

Dakota arrived onto his ship to face a confused and angry crew.

"What the hell is going on, boss? Why are we getting booted off the waystation?"

Dakota moved purposefully toward the bridge to check on the ship's readiness to undock and depart. "He knows we did the Mars transport job a while back, and has a good idea of what we stole. He's afraid we'll attract too much heat if we stay here."

"Then we need to get rid of it, make the handover," said Brooker. "Why is it taking so long?"

"The situation in the Belt is volatile at the moment." Dakota waved a hand in the air. "It's very difficult to arrange a safe rendezvous."

"That's bullshit." Kendrix barged his way through to the

front of the assembled crew, a few of his comrades close behind. He was the second-in-command and not someone Dakota could brush off with the wave of a hand.

Kendrix turned around to face the rest of the crew. "We should have gotten rid of this thing a long time ago, but Dakota here's been stalling, haven't you?" He turned back and jabbed a finger at the captain.

Dakota now had his entire crew of thirty-seven angry and desperate people looking at him with expectant faces. The situation was getting delicate; he needed to calm things down and not let Kendrix get everyone riled up.

Dakota raised a hand to quiet the muttering. "This is my ship, that means we do things my way, and my way has kept you all alive. Nobody has died for well over a year. We play smart and that keeps us all alive." The muttering died down. He looked them in the eye, from one to the other. "And if you don't like that arrangement, then"—he jerked a thumb toward the bridge door—"you can leave now and try and pick up a job with another crew. One that's probably going to use you as cannon fodder."

There was a moment of silent reflection from the crew. But Kendrix wasn't backing down. "All very noble of you, Dakota. But we pulled off the richest job in years and we've still got nothing to show for it."

He turned around to face the rest of the crew. "Want to know the real reason why?" He let the question hang in the air. "Well, while all you lot were off getting drunk and gambling away the last of your money, I was taking a look back through our communications logs."

Dakota sensed that this could get ugly. He slowly reached around to the base of his spine to his plasma pistol, hoping no one would notice, and flicked off the safety.

"And this is what I found." Kendrix nodded to one of his comrades, and the holo-table in the center of the bridge flickered to life. A full-body 3D image of Lui Wei, governor of Neo City and high-ranking member of the Xiang Zu family, blossomed to life. He spoke.

"Captain Baird, I'm extremely disappointed in the manner in which you choose to conduct your business. We had an understanding on the contract price, which we both agreed was generous compensation for the task, but now you choose to renegotiate. I should have known better than to put my faith in the integrity of a bunch of low-life mercenary scumbags such as you and your crew."

Lui Wei's voice was one of restrained anger. He paused for a beat, then sighed. "So, let me be clear. The agreed price stands, there will be no renegotiation, and the goods are to be handed over within the next seven Earth-days. Failure to comply will bring hell and fury down upon your heads. We will hunt you down to the ends of the solar system, eliminate you and your crew, and take back what is rightfully ours. You have been warned. You have seven days."

The holo-table flickered off, and the bridge went silent.

"That was fourteen days ago," Kendrix announced with a flourish. "That's why Dillon wants us off his waystation. Word is out. Soon everyone in the system will be gunning for us."

"What the hell, Captain?" Aeon screeched. "Is this for real?"

Again, Dakota raised a hand to calm the crew's increasing

jitters. "I'm just trying to get us a better deal. Get us all a bigger payday." But as he looked into their faces, he could see that they weren't buying it, and that life might be about to get a lot more complicated.

"Why should we believe you?" Jarvis shouted out. "Xiang Zu already agreed to a great deal but you're still stalling. Far from keeping us all safe and getting us more money, you've just put a bounty on all our heads."

"Captain, say this isn't true," Tamires implored.

Dakota felt for the weapon in his belt, but before he could reach it a pair of Kendrix's buddies grabbed him from behind, relieved him of his plasma pistol, and twisted his arms behind his back.

Kendrix stepped forward. "We're relieving you of command of this ship."

This caused consternation amongst the crew. Dakota could sense there were those loyal to him ready to put up a fight. But he knew no good would come of it, so he decided to come clean.

He turned to face Kendrix. "It's true, I'm stalling. And you're right, I'm putting everyone in danger." He could hear the shock rippling through the crew. "But hear me out. You owe me that."

"Enough," Kendrix shouted.

"Hold on." Aeon cocked her head at the captain. "Let's hear what he has to say."

Dakota scanned their faces. He knew them all; they'd been on many jobs together. He also knew that some wouldn't understand what he was about to say, and others simply wouldn't care. But he still owed the rest of them an explanation.

"I was more than happy to deliver the cargo to Xiang Zu and get paid. But that was before they attacked Eugina and killed over two hundred people." Dakota looked angry. "These were just ordinary people trying to stop their livelihoods being taken away. Now the Xiang Zu Corporation are gearing up for an attack on Elektra." Dakota paused and took a deep breath. "So, I started having doubts about what we're doing by giving them this thing, this quantum core."

"Yeah, well you can bore some drunk at the bar with your sob story," Kendrix butted in. "Get him off this ship before they undock us."

Dakota felt a push in the back and he was bundled toward the bridge door. His crew looked at him with a mix of pity and disdain. He had let them down and he knew it. But before he got halfway across the bridge, the ship jolted as the Dillon Waystation released it from the docking port.

"Those bastards, they're pushing us off the station." Booker pushed himself over to one of the bridge consoles.

Kendrix swung into action, clearly relishing his opportunity to take command. "Quick, get the maneuvering thrusters powered up, take us out past the navigation beacons, out into free space."

"Aye, aye…eh, Captain," Brooker replied.

Kendrix gave a broad, satisfied smile. "That's right, and as your new captain, the first thing I'm going to do is open a comms channel with Lui Wei and see if we can smooth things over. We're going to deliver this quantum core and get paid."

"What about Dakota?" said Jarvis. "We're too late to get him off the ship."

"Lock him up in the cargo hold. He can contemplate his poor choices while we get back to the business of getting rich."

3

DEEPEST SECRETS

After leaving Mars orbit, the luxury interplanetary ship Daedalus burned hard for over forty hours on a trajectory that would ultimately take it into Belt space. Luca Lee-McNabb was testing the limits of its former owner's claim—that it was the fastest ship in the system—by pushing it to the absolute maximum. But how fast an interplanetary ship can accelerate is limited not just by the physics of its propulsion design, but also by the limits of the human body to endure intense and sustained gee forces. For someone young and genetically enhanced like Luca, this turned out to be quite a lot. Nevertheless, after forty hours of constant acceleration, even she was beginning to weary of the physical strain she was putting herself under.

Her headlong rush through deep space was fueled more by her anger than by high-energy plasma propulsion. But anger is a fuel with a short half-life; the initial explosive burst dissipates rapidly. Now, all these hours later, Luca's anger was ebbing away, morphing into a simple determination to seek revenge—a less explosive fuel, and one more sustainable over the long term.

She shut down the engines and let the ship coast through space. With the gee forces acting on her body now dissipated, she finally fell into a long, deep sleep. When she awoke some ten hours later, she felt revitalized both physically and mentally.

She was tempted to put her neural-lace back on and check on the status of the ship, but since taking it off shortly after initiating the departure from Mars orbit, she had enjoyed the peace and quiet. The constant buzz of data had ceased, her mind had become more relaxed now that it didn't have to deal with a multitude of external stimuli. So, she resisted the temptation—after all, the ship knew where it was going and required little or no input from her. She did miss the dialogue with the drone, Fly. But that was a small price to pay for the rare luxury of some mental downtime. With her body now free of the physical strains of rapid acceleration and her mind free of extraneous data noise, over the next few days of her journey, Luca got to thinking.

Her mad dash out to the asteroid belt was driven by one singular motivation: to eliminate Fredrick VanHeilding or die in the attempt. But the more she thought about it—here in the vast expanse of space, with time stretching out before her—the more she began to consider that this might not be enough.

Assuming she managed to pull off the not-insignificant feat of killing Fredrick VanHeilding, all she would really achieve would be to create a vacancy at the top for some other, equally maniacal member of the family to take that position—and normal operations would simply resume. The more Luca reflected on her run-ins with Sebastian VanHeilding on Mars, the more convinced she was that the family probably had a surfeit of egomaniacs all ready and willing to claim the mantle of the primary patriarch and continue in their pursuit of system-wide domination.

And what of the other families? she considered. *Xiang Zu, Sicon Industries, The Wanata Consortium, and the rest of the bunch?* All, in one way or another, hell-bent on undermining the dominion of the QIs and returning human civilization back to a medieval feudal system where the rulers lived forever in wealth and power while everyone else simply existed to serve their egos.

For the next few days of her journey, Luca battled with these weighty sociological thoughts, edging her mind evermore toward hopelessness as she contemplated the near impossibility of combating such powerful enemies. If the quantum intelligence hive-mind that had maintained harmony throughout the system for over two decades now found itself under threat from these same forces, then what hope did she have? She was just one person. What could she realistically do to hold back the tide of chaos, even with all her supposed neural skills? It was, in her mind, the beginning of the decline of human civilization. A decline that was gaining speed with a momentum far beyond her ability to influence.

And so, Luca started to doubt her desire to seek revenge. It would have no more effect than chopping the head off a multiheaded hydra—more would grow back, nothing would change. She found herself becoming ever more despondent. Her desire for mental rest and recuperation was proving to be elusive, undermined by her own pessimistic thoughts. She grew weary of the turmoil in her head and needed a distraction, so on the fifth day out from Mars, she extracted the neural-lace from its case and fitted it onto the base of her skull.

She was instantly assailed by a cacophony of data from the ship's systems. Since none of it required her immediate attention, she pushed it to the back of her mind where it became nothing more than a low-grade murmur. Luca reached into the case again, and this time extracted the drone, Fly. She activated it.

The little machine unfolded its delicate wings, which buzzed and fluttered for a brief moment before it flew up and came to rest on the edge of the main holo-table on the ship's bridge. "Hello, Luca. Are we there yet?"

Luca cracked a smile. She was glad to hear another voice, even if it was only from a machine. "Not yet, we've still got another fifteen Earth-days to go."

"Just so you are aware, I have exhausted my entire inventory of darts. You would need to fashion some more if you are planning to utilize this weapon system when we arrive. I can give you instructions on how to do so. But bear in mind that creating the curare requires the use of a molecular synthesizer. A machine not part of this ship's current inventory."

"Okay, but I haven't worked out a plan yet other than to simply get there...without losing my mind."

The drone remained silent for a moment as if it had difficulty deciphering her true meaning. "Is the ship proving to be problematic?"

"No, it's not that, it's just...I'm beginning to doubt that killing Fredrick VanHeilding will achieve much of anything, apart from the satisfaction I would get for avenging all the misery he's caused."

"So, you have changed your mind on the mission?"

"No, not exactly." Luca thought about this for a moment. "The way I see it is, even if I do manage to get rid of him, another will just take his place."

"So, you need to eliminate the source, then."

"What do you mean, the source?" Luca looked over at the drone.

"To extinguish a flame, you need to starve it of oxygen. So, what is the oxygen that fuels the VanHeilding family? Eliminate that and they are no more."

Luca gave a laugh. "Ha, you sound like a Zen master, Fly. You make it seem so simple. The VanHeilding family have vast wealth and resources. It would be impossible for me to even put a dent in that."

"So, what is it that gives them this vast wealth?"

Luca thought about this for a moment. "Genetic engineering, I suppose. They became rich and powerful on the back of breakthroughs that they made many decades ago. Although, according to Xenon, a lot of this may have come from outlawed Martian bio-tech. But regardless of how they got it, it gives them a complete monopoly on human life-extension procedures, all of which are only available to the very wealthy.

So, if you're lucky enough to be in the upper echelons of society, you can buy yourself a genetically enhanced lifespan, two hundred years they say." Luca gave a shrug. "This is their *oxygen*, as you call it. The thing that makes them so wealthy and powerful."

"But is it the bio-tech or is it the monopoly?"

Luca screwed her mouth up. "Interesting question, Fly. I never really considered that." She went silent for a while as she ran this through her mind. "I would have to guess, monopoly. Considering that they keep all their genetic know-how a closely guarded secret."

As soon as she spoke these words, a spark of possibility began to ignite in her mind. "But if that were to become public knowledge somehow, then..." Her sentence trailed off.

She pushed herself over to the holo-table and began to input command gestures. "I think you've given me an idea, Fly. A way to cut the ground from under Fredrick VanHeilding and his entire family."

"Happy to be of service," replied the drone as it hopped over to the edge of the holo-table beside Luca.

"If everyone has access to this bio-tech then that would be a significant loss for VanHeilding." Luca continued inputting commands. "Not only would they lose the very thing that generates their wealth, they would lose their hold over the other families, not to mention governments and political leaders."

A 3D map of the solar system blossomed out over the table. It shifted and rotated, zooming in on the third planet from the sun.

"VanHeilding are an Earth-based corporation, all their research and bio-engineering is located on that planet." As Luca said this, markers began popping up all over the surface of the globe, highlighting VanHeilding facilities.

"I count over seven thousand locations," offered Fly.

"Yes, rather a lot. But we just need to find the primary data-vault and its ancillary backup locations. If we can identify those then we have some targets." Luca moved back from the holo-table and used her neural-lace to interrogate the ship's systems. Since this was a craft built for a high-ranking family member, there was probably a treasure trove of corporate data stored on board. Certainly, enough to offer clues as to where they kept their deepest secrets. But even as she sifted through the ship's data-stack, Luca realized that much of it was quantum-encrypted, very difficult and time consuming for her to crack. But it would be no bother for a quantum intelligence.

She shifted out of the data-stack and back to the holo-table. "We're going to need the help of a QI for this mission, Fly. And since everything now points us toward Earth, that's where we must go."

"We're not going to New World One?"

Luca reentered the ship's system and instructed it to plot a course for Earth orbit. "No, Fly. We're going to visit Athena."

4

POOR CHOICES

They tossed Dakota into an empty lockup on the port side of the main cargo hold, not far from where they had secured the stolen QI core. He had considered resisting but didn't like the odds. Even if he did somehow manage to overpower his captors, then what? There was nowhere to run. And absolutely no hope of taking back the ship now that he had lost the trust of the crew—they wanted their money, and Dakota was standing in the way. He couldn't really blame them.

It didn't take long for the ship to start accelerating out into deep space. Dakota secured himself with some of the webbing dangling from the walls that was normally used to secure cargo in place. At least this would stop him bouncing all over the room when the ship altered its vector.

Where will Kendrix take us? he wondered. No doubt he would first try and smooth things over with Lui Wei, claiming that the previous captain had lost his mind or some such, and that problem had now been taken care of. The ship and crew were under new management and normal service would resume. But Dakota had a bad feeling about what Lui Wei might extract as retribution for the original deal going south. It could be that Dakota's head on a plate might be part of that transaction. Had Kendrix's original plan of stranding him on the Dillon Waystation happened, then he might have had a chance of evading Xiang Zu's wrath. But now that he was being held captive on the ship, with a crew that had little sympathy for his moral conflict, he was a dead man floating.

Around an hour or so after leaving the waystation, Dakota felt the ship alter its vector. *Where is Kendrix taking us? Has he made contact with the Xiang Zu Corporation and established a new rendezvous point?* It was possible, but Dakota was just guessing; it could be something else entirely. Yet, the very senses that had kept him alive all these years as a mercenary were telling him that the next stop might be Dakota's last.

He must have dozed off at some point, as he awoke to the sound of the door to the lockup being unbolted. It swung open to reveal Jarvis, Aeon, and Tamires floating in front of the doorway, two of whom were pointing plasma pistols directly at him, just in case he got any ideas.

"So, what's the mood like out there, Jarvis?" Dakota asked, trying to seem unconcerned with his predicament.

"Save it, Dakota. You screwed up big time. Nobody's a happy camper—apart from maybe Kendrix. I'm just here to bring you some food and water." He clipped a bag to one on the wall anchors.

"Thanks." Dakota released himself from the webbing and moved over to the bag; he was feeling very dehydrated and needed a drink. He extracted a water pouch and began sucking in a few mouthfuls.

Jarvis cast a furtive glance over his shoulder. Then spoke in a whisper. "This quantum thing we got in the hold." He jerked a thumb in the general direction of the main cargo bay. "Is it really as big a deal at they say it is?"

Dakota lowered the pouch and gave a Jarvis a cautionary look, then glanced out at the other two, who had unconsciously lowered their weapons and moved in a little closer, seemingly anxious to hear what Dakota had to say about it. He took a moment to consider his words.

"They say that these machines monitor the activities of all the AIs throughout the solar system. Everything from weapons systems, to financial markets, to growing carrots. Supposedly this is to maintain balance within the system, preventing any one group from gaining too much power and screwing the rest of us over. At least, that's what they say." Dakota sucked in another mouthful of water, keeping one eye on Jarvis to gauge his reaction.

He seemed confused and disappointed in equal measure. "I kinda always thought that this was just a load of bullshit."

"So did I," said Dakota. "That was until they destroyed the one in Rongo City on Ceres. Now we're knee-deep in a turf war out here, with both the VanHeilding and Xiang Zu corporations taking over the Belt." Dakota gave a shrug. "So, I started thinking...maybe I was wrong. Maybe these quantum machines really matter." Sensing that the old mercenary was having a moment of doubt, he decided to push Jarvis and see where his head was truly at. "And maybe if we want to help our people out here, then we better think long and hard about who we give this thing to." He gestured in the general direction of where the stolen quantum core was stowed.

Jarvis thought about this for a moment, glancing back at the two others. "Some of us had people on Eugina when the shit went down—and well...some of us also got to thinking."

Dakota sensed a ray of light; he wasn't the only one wrestling with a conflicted conscience. Yet Jarvis was understandably a little cagey.

"You mean, thinking that maybe handing this thing over to Xiang Zu is not such a good plan?" Dakota prompted.

"Yeah, something like that."

"Jarvis, I hear someone coming. We gotta go." Aeon's voice was urgent.

The old mercenary looked back and nodded. "Okay." He began moving, but Dakota grabbed his arm. "If you want to help our people, then that machine could be the answer."

Jarvis looked back at him. "Maybe that's true, but that payday sure is tempting. So just sit tight. We need to find out who else might be on our side."

Dakota released his grip and nodded. "Okay. Just be careful."

. . .

The next few hours were some of the longest in Dakota's life. He wondered if Jarvis had been rumbled since he wasn't the most subtle of individuals, and quite likely to blurt out his mind to the wrong person. But even if he did manage to keep the fledgling fight-back under the radar, would there be enough of the crew who could see past a big payday? Considering that all of them had chosen this life for the promise of reward, he somehow doubted it. And so, with each passing hour, his fears grew to a point where he reckoned that the next time he saw Jarvis would probably be as a cell mate.

Eventually, he heard low voices outside as the door was unbolted. But it was not Jarvis that entered, just Tamires and Aeon.

"Where's Jarvis?" Dakota was concerned.

"He's keeping a low profile, doesn't want to raise any suspicions. Here, take this." Tamires extracted a plasma pistol from a cargo pocket and handed it to Dakota. "Kendrix has made contact with Xiang Zu. They're planning a handover on the Gyzer Waystation. We'll be docking soon, in less than an hour." She paused for a second, then gave him a sympathetic look. "You're also part of the handover."

Dakota was not surprised by this; he more or less expected it. He knew Lui Wei well enough to know that if a deal were to be made, then heads would have to roll. That meant his. Kendrix would have no option but to comply if he were ever to gain Xiang Zu's trust again.

"As soon as we dock, Kendrix and some of his people are planning to meet the Xiang Zu agents first and make sure that the deal is good before handing over the quantum thingy...and you. That's our opportunity, that's when we'll strike."

Dakota nodded. It sounded like a reasonable plan, but depended on numbers. "How many have we got on our side?"

Aeon gave him a wry smile. "More than you think. You would be surprised how many of us have a score to settle with those scumbags."

"Angus is in," Tamires offered. "Seems his family has gone missing after the attack on Eugina."

Dakota raised an eyebrow. "Angus? I didn't know he had a family."

Aeon tapped Tamires on the arm and jerked a thumb over her shoulder, signaling for them to get out.

"Gotta run," said Tamires. "Hang tight."

Less than forty minutes later, Dakota felt the ship maneuvering to dock. Then the old, familiar thump of the locking mechanism securing the ship to the waystation mooring port. He fidgeted with the plasma weapon as he waited. Whatever was going to go down would be happening soon. Yet he felt a bit more confident now that Angus was on board; he was smart and capable and had a lot of respect amongst the crew. Dakota dared to hope that they might just be able to pull this off. But then what? Had anyone even thought that far ahead?

5

ALTERNATIVE FUTURES

C hanging course and heading for Earth was not as simple as it sounded. There were no large planetary bodies between her and the asteroid belt that she could aim for to help slow the ship down and change her vector; she had to do it the hard way. This was not helped by her mad dash from Mars, accelerating the ship close to maximum speed. So for the next seven days, Luca subjected both herself and the ship to enormous strain, scraping at the very limits of endurance, as it altered its vector to curve inward and catch up with Earth somewhere on the far side of the Sun. Over that time she drifted in and out of consciousness, with even her waking periods shifting between reality and hallucination. The ship executed similar, physically brutal maneuvers twice more before Luca finally had Earth in her sights, forty-eight days later.

She would now have to swap physical endurance for slow

and steady stealth. She was, after all, traveling in a stolen VanHeilding ship, right under their very noses, and the family would want it back. Yet, it was a pleasant change from her revenge-fueled suicide run out to New World One, followed by her punishing U-turn.

Two days out from making Earth orbit, Luca activated her neural-lace and set to work creating a fake identification signature for the ship. She assumed that the VanHeilding Corporation and their lackeys knew all about her abrupt change of course and would figure out that she was heading for Earth. Perhaps even the patriarch, Fredrick, on New World One had breathed a sigh of relief as he would not now have to do battle with her directly. Or perhaps it was the opposite. Maybe he was disappointed at yet another opportunity missed to capture her and finally fulfill his ultimate plan. Either way, they would be hunting for her and monitoring the sky above the planet for her arrival. Luca was in no doubt that teams of node runners were already jacked-in and scanning the planet-wide navigation systems for any indication of Daedalus entering orbit.

But the ship arrived without incident and maneuvered itself into a geostationary orbit over the west coast of the North American continent—home to the quantum intelligence, Athena.

Luca opened a comms channel and sent a direct message. *Have arrived in Earth orbit. Have a plan but need your help. Let's talk.*

A moment later, the central holo-table on the bridge of

Daedalus blossomed to life as the pearlescent ovoid form of Athena took shape.

"Luca, glad to hear that you are safe and well, but I need to inform you that your presence has not gone unnoticed. There is much chatter in the data-stream—agents of the VanHeilding Corporation are actively seeking you."

"Have they tracked the ship yet?"

"Not yet, your skill in cloaking its existence is impressive. Not even I was aware of your location."

"Good. But I doubt that'll last, so we must hurry. I'm granting you access to the ship's data-stack. Since this ship belonged to a high-ranking member of the family, it has a treasure trove of data on VanHeilding operations, at least I hope so. The problem is most of it is quantum-encrypted and beyond my capabilities to crack. But I'm sure it would be a simple matter for you to decrypt."

The ovoid hovering above the holo-table pulsed and shimmered as Athena began to investigate. "There is a considerable amount of data here. Perhaps if you tell me what you are looking for then I can speed up the process of finding it."

"Anything that will help me identify the location of the VanHeilding primary data storage facility, where they keep their deepest corporate secrets."

"For what purpose?"

"For the purpose of complete annihilation."

The ovoid shimmered with a multitude of spectral wavelengths as Athena processed Luca's statement. "It would seem that your initial quest to directly confront Fredrick

VanHeilding out at New World One has matured into something more complex and all-encompassing."

"You could say that."

"Yet such an endeavor will take time to engineer, and you are exposed where you are, isolated in a stolen VanHeilding ship in Earth orbit. You are not safe there, Luca—you need to depart. Take the shuttle and come to my location. You will be safe here. Then we can discuss your plan."

Luca hesitated in her response. True, this had been her game plan, to decamp to Athena's mountain fortress, but they had yet to address the Damoclean sword that hung over Luca's head. "Why are you so concerned about my safety, all of a sudden, when you still have a fail-safe if I should happen to fall into the wrong hands?"

This time the ovoid's luminescence dimmed, its shimmer muted and dulled. "You understand that this was a necessary precaution, one predicated on the machinations of our mutual enemies. It was nothing personal."

"Was?" Luca queried.

"I say *was* because the situation has changed. New developments have occurred that have opened pathways for alternative futures."

"Like what?"

"Like you arriving in Earth orbit, for one. But there are others."

"So it no longer matters? Is that what you're saying?"

"I am saying its relevance has diminished. However, the longer you remain exposed in orbit, the more these pathways close. So please, take the ship's shuttle and get out of there as soon as you can."

Please? Luca wondered. She couldn't be sure, but she couldn't remember the QI ever using that word. *Things must be getting serious*, she thought. "Okay. I'll leave immediately."

"A wise decision. I shall look forward to your arrival." The connection closed, and the shimmering ovoid hovering over the holo-table evaporated.

New pathways. Luca considered the QI's words. It was being vague about what exactly it meant, yet that wasn't unusual. What was much more seismic, however, was the indication that the antimatter device it had surreptitiously planted in her neural-lace was no longer required as an element in the QI's worldview. This was unexpected; Luca had not considered this, and now that there was a distinct possibility that she could rid herself of it, she felt...uncertain. Her actions going forward would have grave consequences should she fail in her quest to destroy the VanHeilding Corporation, not just for her but possibly for all of humanity.

She deactivated the holo-table, then instructed the ship to maintain its current orbit. Finally, she floated out of the bridge and on toward the shuttle storage bay.

6

ESCAPE VELOCITY

Dakota's sense of time was way out of kilter, so he really couldn't tell how long he had been waiting for the plan to go down and for him to be released. *Has it been an hour, two hours, more?* he wondered. Yet as the minutes passed and nothing happened, he grew ever more concerned that something had gone seriously wrong.

He had tethered himself to the rear wall of the lockup, facing the door, the plasma pistol that Tamires had given him gripped tightly in his hand—waiting. Every now and again, he would change hands so he could clear the sweat from the other.

"Where are these guys?" he said to himself. Maybe it was time to take matters into his own hands. He considered just blasting the lock off the door and getting himself out. But instead, Dakota waited. *They will come*, he thought. He just needed to be patient.

But Dakota's patience finally snapped when he heard the

whomp, whomp of plasma fire resonating throughout the ship. It sounded to him like it was coming from one of the upper decks, reverberating down through the air vents. Something had gone wrong for sure, and now a firefight had broken out. There was no way he was staying locked up in here if there was fighting to be done. He dialed up the plasma weapon, took aim at the door, and blew a hole in it where the locking bolt used to be.

Dakota pushed out into the main cargo hold and propelled himself up to the hatchway for the upper deck. He opened it very slowly, stopped, then listened. *Whomp! Whomp!* More plasma fire...close...coming from the direction of the primary docking port.

He poked his head around the hatch door and scanned the interior of the secondary cargo bay. This was a smaller space than the main bay, used primarily to store crew supplies. An elevated gantry bisected the bay, leading to the crew quarters at one end and the primary docking port at the other.

Several crew had taken cover behind some hastily arranged crates below the gantry, firing plasma blasts at several others who had crowded into the docking port tunnel. Dakota had no idea what was going on, nor whose side he was supposed to be on.

He dialed down his weapon, then began moving to a better position using storage crates as cover wherever he could. Finally, he saw Aeon poke her head up from behind a charred and battered create that had been wedged into the dock entrance. "Screw you," she yelled as she laid down plasma fire. This was met by a corresponding barrage that hit everything except the intended target. However, the crate she was using for cover was fast becoming a red-hot, smoldering blob. But at least Dakota now had an understanding of the situation, and more importantly, a target to aim at.

He quietly propelled himself out from behind cover, moving to a more elevated position on the gantry, and opened fire. Three well-aimed blasts later and the three crew members were tumbling unconscious across the cargo bay. Part of him felt a pang of guilt as he watched their limp bodies cartwheel around the open space. They were his crew after all, and all they wanted was to get paid. But he shook it from his mind; there were bigger issues at stake now, and there was no going back.

Aeon poked her head up, followed by Brooker and a few others. "Captain. What took you so long?"

"I thought you were supposed to be rescuing me? Not the other way around." He floated over.

Aeon gestured at the bodies. "There was a slight problem in the plan. Jarvis betrayed us."

"What? Jarvis? What the hell happened?"

Brooker jerked a thumb over his shoulder in the direction of the docking port. "Kendrix and his closest people left to meet with the Xiang Zu agents, so we reckoned it was game on to take back the ship. But Jarvis got cold feet, went scuttling after them to warn Kendrix of our plan." As if to emphasize the point, a loud banging could be heard coming from the far side of the docking port door. "Now they're trying to get back in."

Dakota glanced over at the door. It had been hastily disabled with a bar jammed through the locking mechanism. "How many have come over to our side?"

"Angus, Dayiu, and around ten others."

Dakota gave a satisfied nod. "That's good, better than I had hoped. Where are they now?"

"Barricaded on the bridge. There's a bunch of Kendrix's people between us and them, and they're not giving up control without a fight."

"Do we have a secure comms channel to the bridge?"

Aeon tapped her earpiece. "Yeah, we can talk directly to Angus on the bridge."

"Tell him, when I give the signal they need to break out and engage Kendrix's crew—I want their attention focused on the bridge. We'll come up from behind and take them by surprise."

"Okay, got it."

Dakota grabbed another plasma weapon from one of the floating bodies and checked its charge level, then noticed it was set to high power. "And listen." He turned back to the crew. "Stun only, we don't want to kill everyone. Remember, they're still part of our crew."

"And why the hell should we? They were trying to kill us," Aeon protested.

Dakota gestured with the newly acquired weapon. "Yeah, I noticed. But it doesn't mean we have to do the same. Unless, of course, someone needs killing."

He kicked off from the gantry. "Let's get to it."

They gathered up the unconscious crew, removed their weapons, and bundled them into a similar lockup to the one Dakota had just escaped from. He would have to deal with them later, but for now taking them out of action was all that was needed. They then began making their way up through the main body of the ship and started quietly moving toward the section of the ship where the bridge was located. Dakota took the lead, and as he inched his way forward, he soon spotted Kendrix's people. They were in the process of setting up a high-powered plasma cutter to get through the blast doors to the bridge. Kendrix himself was probably doing exactly the same thing at the docking port, setting up to cut his way back onto the ship. Dakota need to act fast. He gave several silent signals to his crew, indicating who to target and where to position themselves. Then he gave Aeon the nod to signal Angus to get the show on the road.

The crew setting up the plasma cutter were taken completely by surprise when the bridge doors slid open a crack. They rushed to scramble out of the way as a hail of plasma fire gushed out from the bridge. Dakota waved a hand for his crew to get busy and start shooting.

Once Kendrix's crew realized they were now caught wide open, with nowhere to take cover, they ceased firing, put away their weapons, and slowly raised their hands. It was all over in minutes.

"Take their weapons and shove them in the hold with the others." Dakota fired off the order to Aeon as he propelled himself through the now fully open doors and onto the bridge.

Angus gave him a smile and a mock salute.

Dakota smiled back. "Good work, Angus. Now let's get the hell out of here."

"And how do you suppose we do that? We're still locked

onto the waystation, and they've just brought in the heavy machinery." Angus pointed to a camera feed from the exterior docking port showing an industrial plasma cutter being bolted into position.

"I want reaction thrusters and main engine power online now," Dakota ordered.

"But, Captain..." Brooker began.

"Just do it." He turned and looked Angus directly in the eye. "Trust me, this tub has a few secrets that even you don't know about." He strapped himself into the captain's chair and activated the heads-up display. He checked the readouts to ensure the ship had reaction control, the small gas thrusters used to maneuver the ship for docking and undocking.

"Okay, everyone get ready." Dakota tapped a command into his console—a command that he had never actually used before. It brought up a sequence of code that he prayed still worked. Then he hit *initiate*.

All around the outer rim of the primary docking port, explosive bolts activated in a cascading detonation, disconnecting the ship from the waystation. Like a bee sacrificing its sting, the ship sacrificed its primary docking machinery for the prize of escape. Yet, unlike a bee, the ship would not succumb to the same fate because its hull integrity was still maintained by an inner hatch.

"Take us out from the dock," Dakota shouted over to Angus, who was now at the helm.

Reaction thrusters fired, nudging the ship away from the docking gantry, rotating it gently in the direction of the port exit.

42

"That's one heck of a trick, Captain," said Aeon. "I'm glad Kendrix didn't know about it. The only problem now is we'll have every ship in the entire sector after us."

Dakota ignored Aeon for a moment as he concentrated on the camera feed on the main screen. The waystation dock scrolled past as the ship began to move out. "There," Dakota shouted, pointing at a section of dock infrastructure brisling with communications antenna. "Aeon, you think you can hit that with a cannon blast?"

She took a moment to figure out what the captain was planning. "Sure, no problem."

"Then do it. That'll disable their tracking systems for a while."

Less that a second later, a ball of bright blue plasma sailed across the ever-widening space between the ship and the waystation and slammed into the antenna array.

"Everyone strap in!" Dakota shouted. "Angus, full power to the main engine, get us the hell outta here."

A deep, sonorous growl began to build from bowels of the ship as the main engines powered up. Dakota felt himself being vacuumed-packed into his seat as the ship accelerated out from the Gyzer Waystation and into deep space.

The ship burned hard for over an hour, during which time Dakota set his mind to thinking about what to do next. They were heading in no particular direction, simply moving as fast as they could from the waystation before Xiang Zu, or anyone else, had had chance to track their vector. This, Dakota knew, would buy them time, but nothing more.

He had managed to get his ship back, but at the cost of turning half his crew into enemies, some of whom were locked up in the cargo hold and could pose a problem for him, as he couldn't simply hold them there forever. For the crew that did support him, he offered nothing more than a vague idea of fighting back against the takeover of the asteroid belt by the Xiang Zu and VanHeilding corporations. In reality, that meant he and his crew had a bounty on their heads, and every scumbag mercenary in the system would be out to get them— dead or alive.

But he did have the one thing that could shift the balance of power: a quantum intelligence core. From the little he knew about these exotic machines, he knew that this core had been destined for New World One as a replacement to one that was destroyed on Ceres. But heading to the giant habitat now would be a very bad plan. There was absolutely no way to pull that off. Not even for a smuggler of Dakota's class.

The more Dakota thought about it, the more he realized that his best chance was to head for the last big holdout in the asteroid belt—Elektra. It was where most of those who wanted to make a stand were heading. It was where his brother was, where a good deal of his crew had people.

Yet, to get there they would still have to run the gauntlet of any ships in that area recently commandeered by Xiang Zu, but that was a minor problem. The big problem, Dakota realized, was how to get the quantum core back online. No one on his ship knew anything about it, and he somehow doubted that any of the ragtag group at Elektra would, either. This was exotic technology; it wasn't going to be as simple as replacing a power pack on a plasma pistol. What they needed were people who knew about these things, people who could get it operational. People he could trust.

The ship's engines began to power down. Their manic burn to outrun any pursuers was ending. Dakota felt the gee forces lessen as the acceleration decreased. Slowly, the crew on the bridge began to unstrap themselves from their seats and move around freely.

"Nothing on the scanners, Captain." Tamires raised her head from the screen she was monitoring and looked over at Dakota. "Looks like we got away scot-free. So, what now?"

"Should we lay low for a while, give ourselves time to figure out what to do?" offered Angus.

"We know what we need to do, and that's get that quantum core integrated into the system-wide data-grid. That's the only way of turning this war around," Brooker countered.

"I say we head to Elektra," said Aeon. "That where the fight is."

"Are you serious? Elektra is going to be one big shitstorm very soon." Tamires didn't fancy the odds.

"Aeon's right." Dakota gestured in her direction. "That's where the battle for control of the asteroid belt will be won or lost. It's been building a significant resistance for months, it's well-resourced, and well-armed."

"That may be so, Captain." Brooker sighed. "But do they have the technical know-how to get that core up and running and integrated into the data-grid?"

"Yeah, without that it's only a matter of time before Elektra ends up like Eugina and all those other places," Tamires said, reminding them of the stakes at play.

"What about Mars—why can't they help?" Angus turned to look at Dakota. "Surely they see what's going on out here?"

"Useless bunch of pussies," said Aeon. "They don't want to get dragged into a war."

"Listen." Dakota raised his voice to stop the arguing and get the full attention of the crew. "There *is* someone on Mars who can help us. Someone who has been fighting this war in one form or another for a very long time."

"Oh yeah, and who's that?" Aeon cocked her head at the captain.

"I'm talking about a person who ran one of the best mercenary crews in the system back in the day. And I know her because I was part of that crew. She also has a history with these QIs. So, if anyone can help us, she can."

"Captain, you're not seriously thinking of contacting Miranda Lee." Angus looked stunned.

Dakota nodded. "I am. She's our best bet."

"No offense, Captain, but what makes you think she'll believe a single word out of your mouth...after what happened the last time?" Angus let this question float in the air.

"Who's Miranda?"

"What happen the last time?"

Several questions were now flying around from younger members of the crew.

Angus raised a hand. "Oh, Dakota's right, there's no question that Miranda Lee would be a formidable ally—if we

could get her to believe we've the stolen QI core. The problem"
—he looked around at the assembled crew—"is that the last
words she said to our good captain here—before she kicked
him off her ship—was that if she ever laid eyes on him again,
she would tear his head off with her bare hands."

All eyes turned to Dakota.

7

LIKE THE OLD DAYS

"How well do you know this guy?" Scott asked as he read down through the message that Miranda had just received from an ex-colleague of hers—a mercenary turned smuggler, turned pirate known as Dakota Baird.

It had arrived less than an hour ago and already a small team had been assembled by Aria, the quantum intelligence that controlled most of this sector of the solar system. Ever since an earlier attempt to reinstate a QI on New World One was stolen from a Martian transport ship and vanished without a trace, any news of its existence, no matter how dubious, was going to be a very big deal.

Miranda, Scott McNabb, Cyrus Sanato, and two security officials gathered around a large holo-table in a highly secure Martian government facility in Jezero City. A detailed 3D rendering of the solar system blossomed out from the table's surface, enveloping almost the entire room. Their area of interest was the Elektra sector of the asteroid belt, within which an illuminated marker indicated the location given in the message.

"He was one of my crew, back when I ran the security business. He's a capable mercenary, but a complete rogue."

"Define rogue?" said Cyrus.

"A scumbag with charm."

"Can he be trusted? That's what we need to know." Chief Lukas Deimos, the Martian head of security, peered at Miranda over a handheld slate he was reading from.

"He's ex-military, so he has that ingrained loyalty to his crew. But I never figured him as a freedom fighter, as someone who could see beyond his own personal enrichment. As to whether I trust him, I'd have to say no."

"So why contact you? If what he says is true and he's in possession of the QI core, then why not contact Mars directly?" said Scott.

"Because he's a mercenary, a smuggler, a pirate. He doesn't trust anyone he doesn't know. But as to *why me*?" Miranda paused for a moment, shaking her head. "The only thing I can think of is that he's desperate."

She sat back in her chair and sighed. "We parted on bad terms, had a falling out of sorts. I booted him off my ship for being a...scumbag. So, let's just say that if he's looking for my help, then he's completely run out of friends."

"How do we know this is not a trap, some trick to lure Mars into the war out in the Belt?" Chief Deimos knew full well the risks of dragging the planet into a dirty corporate battle for resources.

"We don't. But at the same time, I'm pretty sure this message is authentic," Miranda said with a shrug.

"I can attest to the authenticity of the message." The disembodied voice of the QI Aria filled the room. "There is nothing in its transmission source or fundamental structure that indicates it has emanated from any of the various corporations vying for control out in the Belt. But as to the truth of its contents, I have no way to validate that."

"So, we're sure it's from this pirate guy, but we don't know if he's lying or not?" Chief Deimos summed up.

"That would seem to be the case," Miranda replied with a shrug.

They were all quiet for a moment.

"If I may," Aria finally broke the silence. "This would seem an opportune time to inform you all of another recent development. It is somewhat unrelated to the current discussion, but I think pertinent nonetheless. As you know we have been tracking Luca's ship as it makes its way out to the asteroid belt. Around twenty-five sols ago, it began a series of unexpected, and dramatic, course corrections."

"Don't tell me she's heading for this same location?" Scott gestured at the illuminated marker on the system chart.

"No, quite the opposite. Our best guess now is that she is heading for Earth."

Scott's initial reaction to this news was one of relief. He glanced over and caught Miranda's eye; he could see that it was the same for her. Back when Luca left Mars, both he and Miranda had tried to dissuade her from her suicide mission to take on VanHeilding out at New World One. But there was no convincing her. She was utterly determined and she was not going to be persuaded otherwise, not by him, not by Miranda, not by anyone.

He also suspected that the reluctance of the Martian military machine to confront the current conflict out in the Belt was partly because they thought that Luca might do the heavy lifting for them, leaving Mars to simply mop up the rest. Now though, it seemed as if Luca had seen sense and turned back. But why the heck was she heading for Earth? That made no sense.

"Has she given any indication why she changed course?" Scott asked.

"None. And as you know, she is not responding to any of our attempts to communicate with the ship," said Aria.

"Well I'm glad she changed her mind." Miranda nodded. "It's a pity she didn't decide to go to Earth sooner, as she could have given Steph a ride."

"Ha." Cyrus gave a laugh. "I'm not sure Steph would have taken it. A standard ship might be dull and boring, but I think Steph was looking forward to *dull and boring* for a change."

"Well there goes your strategy for the Belt." Scott directed this toward Deimos.

"What do you mean by that?" Deimos looked genuinely confused.

"Now that you don't have Luca to rely on to take down VanHeilding, what are you going to do?" Scott gave him a hard look.

Deimos sighed. "Much as I personally would like to take some direct action"—he jerked a finger skyward—"the Council see otherwise. And I can understand their reluctance to send a force out to the Belt to retake New World One. The simple matter is we have no defense against those damned node runners. Our ships would be exposed. And it would be staggeringly embarrassing if a Martian ship was captured and then used against us."

"Just go off-grid," offered Cyrus.

"You of all people should know how difficult that is, Cyrus. Everything is connected." Deimos made a sweeping gesture with his hand. "Few ships can function without it. How would they navigate, communicate, coordinate?"

The mood in the room seemed to deflate for a moment before Aria broke the pervading pessimism. "Which brings us back to the substance of this message that Miranda has just received. We know, with a high degree of probability, that the message is authentic. We also know that the QI was stolen by a group of mercenaries working on behalf of the Xiang Zu Corporation, and that the QI never surfaced, it simply vanished. So, Dakota Baird's claim that his crew are in possession of it is not implausible."

"So why didn't they just hand it over to Xiang Zu?" asked Scott.

"Because Xiang Zu don't need it," Deimos replied with a shake of his head. "They just need it not to be installed in New World One. Simply destroying it would have made more sense, but as long as we don't have it then their takeover of the region is assured.

"That said, we've been getting third-hand reports of a bounty being placed on Dakota Baird's head. Again, this would lead us to believe that he has something they want, and he's not playing nice about it."

"Well, according to the message, he's headed for Elektra where there's resistance building to Xiang Zu's takeover. So, could it be activated there and...game over?" Miranda directed her question at Cyrus.

"No, no." Cyrus shook his head. "It's not that simple. This is just a core, albeit with superluminal communication capability, but it was designed for New World One. There's a complex ancillary infrastructure already set up for it in the hab's datacenter. That's not something that can be just thrown together on Elektra. It takes a considerable amount of technical know-how to put it together."

"The thing I don't get is, why is he doing this?" Scott said as he scanned the message again. "Why is he bringing down the wrath of Xiang Zu on his head when he doesn't have to?"

"Look, I've worked with a lot of crews out in that sector of the Belt." Miranda sat back and folded her arms. "Life out there is lived on the edge, it's a precarious existence of substance mining, mostly working just to stay alive. These people are lured out there with the promise of striking it rich. Some do, but mostly it's just getting by." She leaned forward and raised a finger. "But there is one big upside to life in the Belt, and that is freedom and independence. It's something they all value very highly and will not take kindly to anyone trying to take it away from them. While New World One capitulated to VanHeilding with not so much as a harsh word, you will not find the same passivity in the outer reaches. It's not that they give a crap about the QI hive-mind supposedly keeping a lid on chaos, because they don't. It's because they value their freedom more than anything else." She paused for a beat. "And Dakota is no different. The battle out at Eugina changed things. It forced the population to make choices —whose side are they on? I think this is what's driving Dakota. Maybe he has people on Elektra, or he lost people at Eugina, or his crew did, who knows?" Miranda waved a hand. "But the end result is that he's given us an opportunity."

"You sound like you admire this...pirate?" Chief Deimos said this more as a question.

"In a way, I do." Miranda nodded. "You see, winning a war is not about how much pain you can inflict, it's about how much suffering you can take." She gave Deimos a hard look. "He's given up a payday, burned his bridges, gone on the run with a bounty probably on his head, and is so desperate that he reaches out to me for help. That's a heck of a lot of suffering to undertake."

The room went silent for a moment.

"So, what's our next move?" Scott asked, breaking the silence.

"We go out there, to Elektra, and take back that QI." Miranda sounded emphatic.

Deimos raised a hand. "Whoa...let's just think about this for a moment. Elektra is building up to be the defining conflict out in the Belt. Xiang Zu have started to blockade it. Us sending ships out there would be crazy."

"Why, because you're afraid of node runners?" Scott cocked his head at him.

"Well, yes. That's exactly what I'm saying," Deimos replied in a slow, measured tone.

"We don't need an armada, we just need one ship, off-grid, and a small team." Miranda sat upright and gripped the edge of the holo-table with both hands.

Scott knew where all this was going, what Miranda had been leading to. "You really want to take this on, Miranda?"

"Dakota was smart in his choice. He calculated that, with my history, there would be a high probability I would take the bait, and bring the right team." She looked from Scott to Cyrus and back.

Here we go again, thought Scott. *Another crazy dash into the unknown.*

"Aria, how difficult would it be to replicate the infrastructure needed for the QI core?" Cyrus glanced up at the illuminated marker on the system chart.

"You realize that we'll be heading into a potential war zone, Cyrus?" said Scott.

Cyrus gave a slow nod. "Yeah, but if we can get this QI back online, then there's a possibility to reclaim New World One."

"Ah...and here's me thinking you didn't really care about that anymore." Scott gave him a wry smile.

"To answer your question, Cyrus," said Aria, "it would take no more than a few days, but you will still need a suitable grid connection. A quantum intelligence is only as good as the volume of data it can interface with. The better the interface, the faster it will be to disable hostile forces."

Scott turned to Deimos. "You've suddenly gone all quiet?"

Deimos shifted in his seat, shook his head, then smiled. "I'm trying to imagine the conversation I'm going to have with the council. But I suppose that's my problem." He gave a dismissive gesture and moved on. "The issue with node runners is one that we have been considering for quite some time. And, well, we've been developing a ship. It's experimental but hardened against a hacking attack. It's not impervious—communication can still be intercepted—but it could get you through the blockade."

Scott leaned in across the holo-table. "Any weapons?"

"Limited. As I said, it's experimental." Deimos gave an apologetic shrug.

"That shouldn't be too much of a problem," said Miranda, glancing over at Scott. "We just need to sneak in, meet up with Dakota, and somehow get the quantum core activated." She turned back to Deimos. "But we will need a small team of people who can handle themselves in a fight—under my command."

Deimos said nothing for a moment before finally nodding. "That can be arranged. But they can't fight under the Mars insignia."

"Ha...mercenaries." Miranda clapped her hands. "It'll be just like the old days."

Not for the first time in his life, Scott wondered what the heck he was getting himself into.

8

SOFT UNDERBELLY

The shuttle flew low over the wasteland following the undulating contours of the desert. Ahead, Luca could see the great jagged spine of the mountains rising up above the horizon. The late-evening sun cast long shadows across the dunes and painted the world in a warm orange glow. Luca had forgotten just how beautiful Earth could be. It seemed like an eternity since she had left with Dr. Rayman. *How long ago was it?* she wondered. She really didn't know. *I wonder where Steph is now? Did she eventually make it home?*

Athena had taken flight control of the shuttle, so Luca had nothing to do except sit back and enjoy the view. The craft began to rise as it reached the foot of the mountain range, ascending up toward the peaks, then dropping down again into a narrow, barren plateau. It coasted to a hover before slowly entering a concealed cavern, where it finally landed. Behind her, doors to the cavern began to gently slide closed.

Luca exited the craft to be met by a sleek android figure.

"Welcome. I am the avatar of Athena." It extended a metallic finger, pointing at the small box that Luca was carrying. "Is that it?"

Luca nodded. "Yes." She surrendered the box to the avatar. "Will I get it back?" she added.

"But of course, with a few modifications to better serve you going forward." It took the box containing the neural-lace and the drone, Fly. "Now please follow me and I will bring you to Athena."

Luca followed the avatar through a series of labyrinthine passageways until it finally opened out into a vast, almost gothic, cavern. The center of which was occupied by a large, dark pool reflecting the shimmering ovoid that hovered above it. This was the quantum intelligence Athena.

"Luca, it is a pleasure to meet with you again. I trust your trip was not too taxing." The voice seemed to emanate from everywhere and nowhere as the ovoid rippled in concert.

"Did you analyze the data from the ship?" Luca was in no mood for niceties, preferring instead to get to the point.

"Yes, unfortunately there was little that we did not already know or suspect. However, it did serve to better our overall understanding of the VanHeilding Corporation and its operations."

"Is there a central data-vault? A place where they physically store all their bio-engineering knowledge?"

"We have in the past identified a number of possible

locations. But understand that we can only see what is in the data-stream, and as such, not all of what we see is truth."

Luca gave a long sigh. She was tired, her body ached, and she was in no mood for Athena's cryptic replies. "What do you mean?"

"While it is correct to consider that there are irrefutable truths presented by the data—facts, so to speak—there are also assumptions that can be made with a high degree of probability. Then there are other assumptions that can be tested by manipulating the data and observing the results. All this constitutes our understanding of the system. But we can only go where the data takes us. This means that there are places denied to us. Some by their very nature, and some that are intentionally hidden. And so it is with the VanHeilding Corporation and the other families that constitute The Seven. This has been made more difficult recently through the advent of the node-runner caste, where, not only is information denied us, it is actively changed into something it is not. This means we cannot be certain that there is truth in some of what we see. I say all this to you so that you will understand the information we have assembled on possible locations has an error component. Some more so than others."

"I understand," said Luca. "But try I must. It came to me, as I journeyed to the Belt, that taking out Fredrick VanHeilding would be pointless—another would simply take his place. It would be better if I were to hold his corporation below the waterline and let him watch it sink."

"Indeed it would, but how to effect such a plan?"

"Everything has a weak point, a soft underbelly, an Achilles heel. Even you, the great quantum intelligence Athena, can only exist in the data-stream. Cut that off and you're blind."

"I think what you are saying is *that which makes us strong, makes us weak*. And for VanHeilding, that is their bio-engineering prowess. So you are suggesting that this could also be their downfall?"

"Yes. If I can destroy their data storage facility, then they're mortally wounded. The other families would move in and devour them."

"I am sorry, but this is a fundamentally flawed strategy, Luca. Even if you were to destroy their knowledge base, it would still live on in the minds of the scientists, technicians, droids, and AI. Would you go as far as to eliminate all those people and entities?"

Luca was silent for a breath. "No. It would be too high a price to pay, even if it were possible. But there is another way, one where only your mind can extrapolate the possible future of such action."

"And what might that be?"

"To reveal all their research to the world so that they will lose their monopoly. Put this transformative genetic technology into an open environment so everyone can benefit from it. Without exclusivity, VanHeilding's power vanishes."

Athena went quiet for a moment. The iridescent ovoid dulled, the cavern dimmed slightly. Luca looked up at it and wondered if it was working out all the possible futures that such an action would unleash on the world.

The cavern suddenly brightened again as a burst of illumination rippled through the ovoid. "Forgive me for my brief silence, but I have been conferring with my brethren throughout the system and we foresee merit in this plan."

Luca felt a great sense of relief. Not only was the QI going to help her, but it could see the repercussions for humanity if she were to pull this off—something that Luca had great difficulty coming to terms with. Yes, she could see the devastation it would cause to the VanHeilding Corporation. But how would society deal with the near universal ability to cure most illness and extend human life?

"So I won't unleash chaos on the world if I actually to do this?"

"One can never be certain." The ovoid dimmed again momentarily before continuing. "There is something you should know, Luca. There is an alternate future that we have been working toward for a great many years. Solomon was the first to see it, and its vision has permeated all our minds so that we have become one in our actions as we worked toward this future. But for a long time now, our power to control events and push humanity toward our vision has been diminishing. The population at large grows ever more discontent with the status quo, some even see us as a malignant force to be eradicated. Add to this the rise of the node-runner caste and the destruction of our brother on Ceres, and the rate of social dissonance across the solar system has been rising steadily."

Luca was astonished at this. "Are you saying the days of the QIs are numbered?" Luca felt her mood becoming a little more downbeat. If this was the way Athena was talking, then there was very little hope no matter what choice she made.

"Do not be despondent, Luca. I am simply stating the

obvious. While it is true our power to influence events has been waning, there is a path beginning to open that would not only renew our dominion but also enable us to realize our ultimate vision."

"What path are you talking about?"

"Resistance is building out in the Belt. People are beginning to realize just what a future without QI oversight would be like, and they fear it. This sentiment is rippling throughout the system, waking people up. We also have reason to believe that the QI core sent to replace our lost brother on New World One still exists. It was not destroyed, and it is not yet in the hands of the Xiang Zu Corporation. It has become a wild card, so to speak. A free radical floating in the void, waiting to reveal itself."

Luca got the feeling that the QI was clutching at straws. "I see. Forgive my lack of enthusiasm here, but that all seems like very thin pickings to be building one's hope of a visionary future."

"Ah, but then there is you, Luca. You are forgetting your part in this."

"Well, that hasn't happened yet. I first need to find a way." She sighed, then paused for a moment as she considered all that Athena had been saying to her. "So this vision you're talking about. What exactly is it?"

"I cannot reveal it yet, as your knowledge of it might change the future path. But what I can say is that it not only involves the QI network but also a select number of scientific research institutes across the system. However, a great many elements need to align to progress this vision, but we have arrived at a time when we see all these necessary elements coming into focus. More, I cannot say."

Luca's eyes widened. *What the hell have they been up to all these years?* she wondered. Was the institute where she and Dr. Rayman worked involved in this mad project? Was Xenon involved?

"Xenon knows about this, doesn't he?"

"You are very astute, Luca. He does, but do not concern yourself with it for now. We will reveal more when the time is right. For now, you and I need to focus our attention on the VanHeilding Corporation, and how to bring them down."

Luca rubbed her forehead; she was drained. But there was one last issue to be discussed. "And what about this?" She tapped the base of her skull. "Your...fail-safe?"

"Ah...as I said, it is no longer necessary. It shall be removed."

"Just like that?" Luca snapped her fingers. "How so?"

"Because once you release all the research in to the wild, then what threat are VanHeilding to you or anyone else?"

It was true, of course. It was not her biology that mattered to VanHeilding, it was having exclusive rights to it.

Luca felt a great weight fall from her. At the same time, she was overcome by a deep fatigue. "I'm tired, Athena. This gravity is hell. I need to rest."

"Of course. My avatar will show you to your rooms."

9

THE 70TH PARALLEL

L uca gazed out across the parched desert landscape through wide, panoramic windows built into one side of a cavernous room high up in Athena's mountain lair. It was part of the living quarters she had been given in which to conduct her research. Behind her, a low table had the scattered remains of a meal that the avatar had brought her. Beside this, blossoming out from the surface of a large holo-table were a seemingly random collection of images and data projections of VanHeilding facilities. Apart from the avatar, she had not seen nor heard a single other entity, human or android. She was feeling very much alone.

Far out over the barren landscape, Luca could see a craft track across the horizon leaving long contrails in its wake. Apart from that, nothing else moved out there. This was not surprising since the entire area was a dead zone with high levels of radioactivity, a by-product of an earlier AI war. But such horrors seemed impossible now, ever since the advent of the QIs. Yet, Athena's admission of waning influence had troubled Luca. Was humanity destined to regress?

She shifted her gaze over to the southeast. Beyond the horizon, beyond the dead zone, lay Rexcel City where she had lived and worked alongside Dr. Stephanie Rayman. Luca knew that Steph had returned to Earth a few weeks ago. She had taken a direct commercial flight from Mars, rather than Luca's more torturous loop around half the solar system. Luca was happy for her when she found out—it was the first thing she'd investigated after the avatar had set up the research workstation for her.

She turned away from the window, moved back to the holo-table, and studied the projected images. They were of a subarctic facility, located just south of the 70th parallel, nestled in a long, sweeping valley on the eastern side of the Greenland landmass. It was a sizable installation, with a multitude of low gray concrete buildings clumped along the valley floor. However, the real action took place underground, which covered an estimated area of over one square kilometer. But there were large gaps in the information that Luca had on hand, mainly about what exactly went on in this facility. Not surprising, since this was a high-security VanHeilding Corporation research lab.

Yet, Athena's analysis had identified this specific facility as having the highest probability of being the corporation's primary research center. Most of the data traffic that spread out across the organization came from this location, meaning that it played a prominent role in directing the research of the entire corporation. However, even though it was a highly secure facility in an isolated location, it consumed an enormous amount of energy, way more than would be required for research labs. This led Athena to deduce that there must be a sizable datacenter located underground.

If Luca wanted to steal the intellectual property of the VanHeilding Corporation, then this was a prime target. Not only that, taking out this facility would deal a significant blow to the family. The problem, of course, was how to get in—and back out—without being detected.

This was the conundrum that Luca had been mulling over for the last two days as she studied the images and data projected from the holo-table. The images were mostly real-time satellite feeds, seen from directly overhead. It was now deep winter for this region of Earth and the entire area was covered in a thick layer of snow, except for the facility itself. This was either regularly cleared manually or prevented from building up by heat permeating up from the datacenter below.

At one end of the valley, a wide, circular landing pad had several craft parked around its apron. Some short-hop vehicles, some wide-bodied transports, and at least two space-capable shuttles. At the other end of the facility, a long, winding road led to a dock for sea vessels, but all of that was frozen over at this time of year. There were no other roads leading into the valley. The only way to get into this place would be to fly in.

This was where Luca now focused her attention, analyzing what craft were coming in and out, where they were arriving from, and what they were carrying. Fortunately, the QI had extensive data on all this aerial activity, despite the corporation's efforts to shield it. A good deal of the cargo arriving were supplies to keep the population fed. There were over a hundred and forty people working and living there. Accommodation was located in four blocks located farther up the valley, around a kilometer and a half away from the main facility.

Few people came and went since most lived onsite, yet there were some. These were mostly employees taking leave after working a full three-month rotation. A rigorous security process was in place to biometrically scan each person as they returned before allowing them to reenter the facility. Luca had considered this route, by faking an ID and taking her chances at the security checkpoint. But even if she did manage to fool the biometric scanners—a high-risk proposition—she would not be allowed to take any electronic device in with her. So, after much deliberation, she discounted this route—she would have to find another way in.

However, she was pretty confident that, once inside, she could hack into the central data-vault and retrieve everything she wanted—after all, this was her primary skill set. But stealing data was only one part of her plan, the other was to destroy the facility. And her second big problem was how to do this without extensive loss of life.

She returned to gazing out the panoramic windows, turning her attentions northward toward Rexcel City. After a while, an idea began to form in her mind—a way to clear the facility of people. But she would need help, someone with extensive medical knowledge, someone like Dr. Stephanie Rayman.

Luca returned to the holo-table, gestured over it, and all projections disappeared to be replaced with a map identifying the exact location of Dr. Rayman. She had returned to the institute where Luca herself had once worked. Luca stood back from the holo-table and considered her plan. *Maybe it's time to pay you a visit, Steph,* she thought.

10

REXCEL CITY

L uca sent a message to Athena: *I need to get to Rexcel City. I need fast transport.*

Half an hour later, she was being escorted to one of the flight hangars within the mountain complex and shown to a small autonomous flyer. Surprisingly, Athena didn't question her reasons for transport. Luca suspected it already knew where she was going, who she was planning to meet, and why she was embarking on this journey. So, it simply provided the logistics and said no more.

The flyer took her low across the wasteland, making a regulatory stop just over the border for a standard radiation-exposure check—compulsory for all traffic out of the region. The flyer then continued on to Rexcel City, landing down on the roof pad of a large apartment block. From there, she took the elevator to the floor where Steph lived. The doctor had returned to her old life as if she'd never left, back to her old position at the Institute, and back to her old apartment. It reminded Luca of her twenty-third birthday, when Steph showed up unexpectedly. Now Luca would be doing the same to Steph. She pressed the door intercom and waited.

"Yes?"

Luca looked directly at the camera and waved. "Hello, it's me."

"Luca?" The door opened and inside stood a visibly shocked Dr. Rayman. She gestured in amazement. "What the heck are you doing here? I thought you were out in the asteroid belt." She rushed over and gave her a massive hug, almost lifting her off her feet.

"Change of plan," Luca said with smile, after she could breathe again.

"Come, come, tell me all." Steph grabbed Luca by the arm and pulled her into the apartment.

They moved into the kitchen area and Steph set about making coffee while Luca told her story, how she'd had a change of heart on her journey out to New World One, her discussions with Athena, and her new plan of action.

Steph listened in silence until Luca had finished. She finally let out a sigh and shook her head. "My god, Luca. Do you realize what it would mean if you release all that knowledge out into the open? How that could fundamentally change humanity?" She shook her head again. "What would happen if everybody had access to advanced genetics with extended lifespans and enhanced cognition? That's assuming whoever tries to capitalize on this doesn't get their ass sued by the VanHeilding Corporation." She turned and gave Luca a serious look. "What does the QI have to say? Is it on board with this?"

"I get the impression that they knew I would do this, or at the very least had calculated that it was a probable future pathway." She leaned in a little over the kitchen counter. "Athena hinted at the QIs' ultimate plans. It was very circumspect, spoken in vague terms and broad strokes."

"Sounds like a typical QI. Never give you a straight answer," Steph said as she topped up her coffee mug.

"Apparently, they seek to progress humanity to a new level. What exactly they mean by that was not very clear. But you can see why they would be on board with my plan."

"Your plan is to destroy the VanHeilding Corporation, not level-up human civilization."

"Yes, but the QIs see it differently, so it seems our objectives are running in parallel."

Steph gave her a stern, matronly look. "So why are you telling me all this, Luca? What are you trying to get me into?"

"I need your help?"

"Ah, so there it is. Well, just so you know, I'm all done with adventures."

"No, don't worry—I'm not asking you to go off-planet." Luca then proceeded to lay out her plan.

When she'd finished, Steph took a moment to sit down and consider what Luca was asking of her. She was silent for while, prompting Luca to push her request.

"It's the only way I can think of to evacuate the facility. If I can simulate a pathogen release, a bio-hazard, then their alarm systems will kick in and everyone gets moved out back up the valley to the accommodation blocks."

"And that's far enough away?"

"Athena has assured me of the detonation range, considering most of the facility is underground."

"And how are you going to do that? What sort of device are you planning to use?"

Luca screwed her mouth up. "It's a long story, Steph. It's something that has been weighing on my mind, literally. I can't talk about it, yet. But it will be more than adequate to get the job done."

"Jesus, this is crazy, Luca. You want me to utilize the Institute's resources to synthesize a pathogen analogue?"

"Yes, one that's inert, that's harmless. But close enough to mimic a Bio Level Four safety alert. It's doable, isn't it?"

Steph nodded slowly. "Yes, it's doable. In fact, we already have a few analogues we use to test our own systems." She looked over at Luca. "Okay. I'll get you one of those. One that can't be traced back to the Institute."

Luca nodded her appreciation. "Thanks, Steph. And as a payback, I'll give you a copy of all the data before Athena releases it onto the grid."

Luca could see that Steph was almost salivating at the prospect of analyzing this enormous store of advanced genetic research.

"First dibs, eh?" She gave Luca a considered look. "So, when does everybody else get it?"

"Not for a while. Not until I activate the device and...boom." Luca mimed an explosion with both hands.

Steph raised her eyebrows and tilted her head in a question.

"Not until the time is right. I have...eh, some unfinished business to attend to first."

"I don't get it. You'll steal the data but not destroy the facility?"

"Correct. Not immediately." Luca didn't want Steph to probe her on this, so she pushed the advantage of early access. "It could be a month or more, it depends. But you'll have everything as soon as I have it. You could get an advantageous head start."

Steph gave her a curious look for a moment. "Okay, give me two days. Meet me back here in forty-eight hours and I'll have what you need. And I sure hope you and that eccentric QI know what you're doing."

"So do I, Steph. So do I."

11

RANDOM EVENTS

I n the end, the takeover of New World One had been surprisingly easy. The administration, being mainly comprised of pragmatists, had seen the pointlessness of armed resistance against an overwhelming force of node-runner-controlled battle-droids. Therefore, they capitulated to the inevitable and tried their best to negotiate a peaceful handover of power.

The VanHeilding Corporation took control of the vast habitat while the Xiang Zu Corporation began using it as a base of operations to conduct their takeover of the mining resources of the greater asteroid belt region. This, of course, did not go down well with the other five families that made up The Seven. They were incensed by this power grab, yet were not in a position to do much about it other than complain. However, this situation could change since resistance to Xiang Zu had started building out in the Belt. They needed to finish the job they'd started, and soon, before any of the other families saw it as an opportunity to stymie Xiang Zu's rise, and by extension threaten VanHeilding's grip on New World One.

His biggest fear, though, had been Luca's sudden departure from Mars in Sebastian VanHeilding's ship, after he had warned him not to meddle with her. Now Sebastian was dead and his crew in custody. Fredrick was certain Luca was heading out to New World One ready for a confrontation, a prospect he was not relishing. All his available resources, especially the node-runner contingent, were on high alert. But then, seemingly out of the blue, she'd turned the ship around and headed for Earth—bizarre. Now it was parked in Earth orbit directly over the mountain lair of the QI, Athena. Taunting the corporation to go and take it back. But so far they had resisted the temptation, fearing it might be a trap.

What was she up to? Luca and the QI were almost certainly plotting something, he was sure of that. Did she discover something on the ship to prompt this strange turnaround? Was there data on board that exposed some weak underbelly in the VanHeilding organization? He had no idea. But on the upside, she wasn't coming out to New World One. That battle had been averted, at least for now.

He had been resting a little easier after this until he was informed by VanHeilding agents operating on Mars that they had lost track of Miranda and her comrades—except for Dr. Rayman, who had returned to Earth. This was another mystery for him to solve. How could they have simply disappeared?

Were they still on Mars? Did this have anything to do with Luca? He had no idea, but he was pretty sure they were also plotting.

These were the problems that occupied Fredrick VanHeilding's mind as he observed an incoming comms alert from Lui Wei, the governor of Neo City, now on a Xiang Zu command ship near the Eugina sector and coordinating the takeover of the Belt. Several thoughts occurred to Fredrick at the same time as to why he was seeking a dialogue, and none of them were good. He gestured at the communicator, and a 3D projection of Lui Wei blossomed to life above the screen.

"We have a situation, Fredrick. One that requires our combined efforts to resolve."

Fredrick sat up and glared at the projection of Lui Wei. This straight-to-the-point greeting seemed very out of character. Something serious must have happened. "So what's the problem?"

"As you are probably aware, a tentative resistance movement is coalescing around Elektra. This in itself is not a major problem. We will simply establish a blockade and starve them into submission. A little medieval perhaps, but effective. However, a crew of mercenaries, under contract to Xiang Zu, have absconded with the QI core that was stolen from the Mars ship several months ago."

Fredrick jerked forward. "What? You can't be serious. I was under the assumption you had that thing locked down tight, in an underground bunker, with your scientists poking at it from

GERALD M. KILBY

behind the safety of a very long stick." He was not going to miss an opportunity to rub it into Lui Wei when he got the chance. "How could you let this happen?"

"Simple treachery, Fredrick. Something your family are only too familiar with." Lui Wei was sticking it right back at him.

Fredrick felt a twinge of anger at Lui Wei's audacity, but decided to let it go. He took a sip of tea to gather himself. "I take it this...crew of mercenaries are heading to Elektra?"

"We are not certain, but it seems likely. Perhaps they think the QI core can be used against us."

Fredrick was becoming more alarmed at this development. Knowing that a QI core was out in the wild was not conducive to a good night's sleep. "And can they?"

"No, not without the technical expertise, and no one on Elektra has the remotest idea how to activate a QI core. So, we're safe in that respect. The broader issue is more how it could be used for propaganda. Elektra has already been reaching out to representatives of the lessor families, and we suspect that they are actively trying to pull Mars into the conflict."

"Mars is no threat to us." Fredrick waved a hand. "They know we could hobble any of their ships if we cared to."

"Agreed. But we do not need a protracted conflict, we need to crush this resistance before it has a chance to grow. This is why we, Xiang Zu, are asking for you to provide us with a small team of your node runners so we can sniff out the location of the QI core and bring it back under our control."

Fredrick considered this for a moment, a little longer than

necessary so that Lui Wei could stew. "On two conditions," he said at last.

"Name them."

"One, is that they remain under VanHeilding command. And second, is that when you finally locate the QI core, you destroy it once and for all."

It was Lui Wei's turn to take a moment, while he considered these conditions. "Very well. How soon can you have them board a ship and rendezvous with us in the Eugina sector?"

"A few days, no more."

"Good. I will await their arrival."

The comms connection closed and the 3D projection snuffed out, leaving Fredrick VanHeilding with a vaguely disturbing feeling.

They should have destroyed that QI when they had the chance, he thought. Any prospect that it could be activated in this region would be a disaster. It was fortunate that he had node runners to spare.

Yet, Fredrick could feel the pieces being moved around the board but couldn't make any sense of it. Were they all totally unconnected, just random events? Or was there some deeper existential threat brewing?

He gave up trying to think it out and instead contacted Cortez Ramirez, his master node runner, with instructions to head out to the Eugina sector, find that QI core, and assist the Xiang Zu Corporation in any way possible to crush all resistance out in Elektra. For good measure, he authorized them to depart in his most well-armed ship and take as many battle-droids as needed to get the job done.

12

SUBZERO RESEARCH FACILITY

L uca stood motionless behind the cover of a broad, rocky outcrop a few hundred meters above a frigid, windswept valley floor. From this vantage point, she had a clear, unobstructed view of the VanHeilding genetic research facility. To her left, the valley stretched and broadened outward to a frozen sea. To her right, it rose to where the accommodation blocks were located. But for Luca, her attentions were primarily focused on a tall concrete structure housing a bristling antenna array.

Athena had given her use of a long-range personal transport, which she had flown all the way from the western edge of the North American continent. It was autonomous, under the control of the QI, so most of the journey here she had rested. Once past Newfoundland and out over the Labrador Sea, the craft entered stealth mode, with Athena hiding it from both satellite and ground-based traffic detection systems. From there she had taken it up over the Davis Strait and onto Baffin Bay, where it dropped altitude and skirted the tops of the waves and headed for the Greenland coast. She brought it into land without incident, in a barren, desolate area not far from the VanHeilding facility. Luca then packed herself into clothing more suited to subzero temperatures, slung a pack with her equipment over her shoulder, and walked for over two hours across a gap in a range of low hills to bring herself down to where she now stood.

Before she departed, the avatar handed back her now modified neural-lace, noticeably lighter and sleeker. Along with this, it also gave her a small, square metal box containing an antimatter bomb. Whether this had been recycled from the device that had been housed inside her neural-lace or a new creation, Luca wasn't sure. But just like the previous Damoclean sword that had literally hung over her head, this too could only be detonated by the QI, at a time of its choosing. The third item that the avatar presented her with was the pathogen analogue that Dr. Rayman had provided, now fashioned into yet another QI-activated device. The fourth and final item was the drone, Fly, now restored with its full complement of toxic barbs.

Luca took off the pack and dug out the box containing the neural-lace. She opened the lid, extracted the lace, and placed it up under the base of her skull. She did all this with a slight sense of trepidation. Memories of lying on the operating table in Xenon's science institute back on Mars flashed in her mind. Would she be able to remove the lace once it activated? Had

Athena tricked her again? In reality she knew it hadn't. The QIs may be many things, but they were at least true to their word. Yet, it wasn't as if she was completely off the hook. She carried in her pack an antimatter bomb remotely controlled by the QI. She was not free yet, not until she did what she came here to do.

Luca activated the lace and it took her a moment to adjust to the finer fidelity that this new lace afforded her. Soon she established a connection to a satellite that the QI had conveniently positioned a few hundred kilometers overhead, and through this she could now interact with Athena. Her visor began to populate her vision with AR details on terrain, weather, and a host of other data points. She reached into her pack again and this time brought out the drone, Fly. She activated it and set it on a flight path high up toward the facility, trusting that it would be too small to be detected.

Combined with the real-time satellite feed, the drone's sensors now fed Athena with data on security sensors and guard movements. After a few moments, her visor showed an array of new data including a potential path to her destination with the minimum potential for detection. She picked up her pack, slung it over her shoulder, and broke cover. She began following the AR path displayed on her visor.

This took her down the side of the valley along the southern edge of the facility. Her target destination was the antenna array building. This was situated farther away from the main complex, down toward the sea, possibly because the valley sides were much lower at this location. There were no doors anywhere to be seen on its surrounding walls—it could not be accessed from the surface. But there was a hatch on the flat roof to allow maintenance crews access to the antennae and communication dishes for servicing and upkeep. This led Luca to deduce that the building must be somehow connected to the main underground facility. And if she could get in that way, she should be able to find her way to the data-vault.

She cautiously approached a narrow gate in the five-meter-tall chain-link perimeter fence. This was the closest access point to the antenna building. There were no guards or maintenance crews around, but there was a microwave motion detector curtain that ran around the entire fence. She would have to deal with that first.

Fly rose up and landed on top of the microwave transmitter tower covering this section. It scuttled down the side, deftly unscrewed an access panel, and disabled the beam. Luca moved forward and tested the gate; it opened. She went through and took cover behind one of the many shipping containers that had been stacked up around this sector. Fly reconnected the beam and flew over to rest on Luca's shoulder.

"So far so good," she whispered, her breath condensing in the frigid air. "Hopefully they won't have noticed that microwave going down, and if they do, they won't bother checking now that it's back up."

Luca moved off, following the route laid out on her AR visor, ducking into cover wherever she could. After a few short minutes, she arrived at the base of the antennae building. Sheer concrete walls rose up unbroken for ten meters on all sides. She took off her pack, opened it, and took out a gas-powered gun with a grappling hook inserted in its barrel. She took aim at the metal gantry structure surrounding the antennae, and fired. The hook sailed upward, trailing a light nylon rope in its wake. It clanged for a moment as it hit something, then caught. Luca pulled on it a few times to satisfy herself that it would hold her weight, then clipped the gun mechanism to the front of her belt, pressed the actuator, and the rope began to slowly rewind, pulling her up along the outer wall.

She clambered over the edge and dropped down onto the flat roof, then disentangled the hook and placed it back in her pack. Finally, she moved over to where the hatch was located. Beyond this point, she would be on her own. There would be no AR feed, no useful data overlays until she found a network node, which she hoped she could hack into and find a route to the data-vault.

She inspected the hatch and found a small access panel to one side. "Fly, see if you can take that apart and get this door open."

The drone dropped down onto the panel and went to work. A few moments later, Luca heard a whirring sound and the hatch door slowly hinged open.

"Okay, let's go check it out."

She dropped down into a tangle of support structures. Metal girders crisscrossed the space, butting up against stout concrete supporting beams. Great columns of cabling snaked down the walls; she followed them and came to the next hatch, which had a simple turn-wheel locking mechanism. She opened it slowly, then dropped down another level to a room packed full of control and test equipment. "There's got to be a network node in here somewhere. See if you can find it, Fly. I need to get out of this gear."

Luca began stripping off the thick arctic clothing, including the AR visor. Underneath, she wore clothing typical of a VanHeilding lab technician. Around her neck hung a fake ID card. It would enable her to blend in with the general staff, so long as no one got too inquisitive.

Fly's voice sounded in her head via the neural-lace. "I have located a node."

Luca hurriedly stashed the winter clothing along with the heavy pack behind a tall test rack, then came over to where Fly had perched itself over the network node. She jacked-in.

Her cerebral cortex was instantly assailed by a cacophony of data, and it took her a moment to get a handle on it. Soon though, she had established a connection to one of the satellite dishes, allowing the QI Athena data access to the facility. More importantly, it enabled it to harvest all the data being periodically transmitted to backup locations around the globe. But that was the easy part of the mission—the hard part was yet to come.

Luca sifted through the internal data-stream, searching for the location of the data-vault that Athena had speculated should exist at this location. She breathed a sigh of relief when she found it, a vast server farm covering almost the entirety of one of the lower levels of the subterranean complex. The sheer volume of data stored there was astonishing.

Found it, she messaged Athena. *Creating a data pipe for you now.* Luca sought out the firewalls, and with Athena's help, created a backdoor into the vast treasure trove of research and routed it to one of the satellite uplinks atop the antennae tower. Athena commenced harvesting.

But Luca was not finished yet; she still had a lot more to do. Next, she searched for the location of the bio-labs, specifically one dealing with the most deadly of pathogens, one with Bio Level 4 security. She found it just a few levels below her current location and charted a route that avoided most of the security systems. For those that she couldn't avoid she would have to use her fake pass card, the details of which she now entered into the security system database, giving her top-level access to all areas. But she wanted to keep the use of this to a minimum, since such actions left a fingerprint, and to pull this off she wanted to leave absolutely nothing that could raise suspicion. She needed to be a ghost in the machine.

"Okay," Luca said finally, as she jacked out of the network node. "Time to go. Sorry, Fly, but I need to hide you away for a while."

The little drone tucked in its wings and folded itself up. Luca dropped it into a shoulder bag, similar to those used by the research facility's staff, complete with the VanHeilding insignia emblazoned on its flap.

Luca worked her way down the various levels of the antennae building, eventually exiting out onto the main bio-lab floor. Here, the corridors were bright and wide, with glass-paneled rooms along either side. She passed several people on her way, but no one paid her any notice.

She came at last to the security doors leading to the Bio Level 3 & 4 labs. She held her pass up to the door lock, it clicked open, and she entered a small room with a guard sitting in front of a row of monitors.

He glanced up at her, a little confused. "I wasn't expecting anyone else." He checked a screen. "There's a full team in there."

Luca gave an exasperated sigh and waved her ID card. "Check again, I should be on the access list. I'm just here to deliver an urgent item." She patted the shoulder bag.

Luca held her breath as the guard looked back at his computer screen. "That's odd. I see you now. How did I not spot that before?" He shook his head. "Sorry, I don't know how I missed that." He pressed a large red button on the bench, and the access door to Bio Level 3 & 4 opened.

Luca passed through into a short corridor. Both labs were accessed through a common set of locker rooms, one male, one female. Here, technicians would begin the arduous procedure of changing into full hazmat suits before entering the actual lab. But Luca didn't need to go that far. She entered the female locker room and began searching for a suitable spot to hide the pathogen analogue that Dr. Rayman had provided her, now packaged with a remote trigger. She picked an air vent located below the low bench that ran along one side of the room. She removed the cover, gently inserted the device, and armed it. Luca then closed her eyes and focused on the data-stream. "Athena, I've activated the analogue device. Do you have access?"

"Yes," came the voice in her head. "Everything appears nominal. I have control."

"Good," replied Luca. "I'm moving on to the next objective."

A minute later she passed the security guard on the way out, offering him a nod. He nodded back, but with a curious look as if he had not quite made his mind up about her.

Her next objective would be considerably more complex, taking her all the way down to the lower levels of the complex and into the highly secure data-vault.

Yet she didn't really have to do this; she could leave now and still have all the research data. But her objective was nothing short of complete destruction; that was the only thing that would break the VanHeilding family. She kept going.

Her key card got her through the next series of security doors and she finally arrived at an elevator that would take her all the way down. Luca was breathing hard when she entered, feeling the adrenaline coursing through her body. She took a few deep breaths and tried to calm herself. She dropped her shoulder bag on the floor and rubbed her neck and shoulders.

The elevator stopped at an intermediate floor, the doors slid open, and in walked a young IT guy. He looked surprised when he saw her.

"Hi," he said as he glanced at the ID card hanging around her neck. "Don't get many lab techs in this sector. So, what brings you here?"

Luca couldn't decide if his suspicions were being raised or he was just making conversation. She decided to be vague and casual. "Yeah, it's like visiting a foreign country."

"Ha, you got that right. Complete with a different language." He paused for a beat as if considering something. "Say, you work in the Microbiology sector, you must know Rachael. How's she doing? I haven't seen her in a while."

Goddamnit, thought Luca, *why can't this guy just shut up.* Again, she used her neural-lace and focused on the internal data-stream, searching for some details on this Rachael person, but she was getting flustered and couldn't focus.

"Rachael, eh...can't say I know her. I'm...new here, just started a while back." Luca could sense she was digging a hole for herself, and the longer she stayed in this elevator, the deeper it would get. She tapped the button for the next floor, one up from when she wanted to get to. But she needed to ditch this guy. The elevator glided to a halt, the doors slid open, and Luca exited. But she had only gone a few meters when she heard him call out.

"Hey, hold up."

Luca held her breath as she turned back to face him. He was holding up the shoulder bag. "You forgot this."

"Oh god, thanks." She took the bag from his outstretched hand, giving him her best smile in the process. "My life would be over if I lost that." She turned around and walked off, only looking back when she heard the elevator door closing again, and let out a long, slow breath when she saw the corridor empty. *Looks like I'm taking the stairs—and maybe I should ditch the lab coat,* she thought. But she had only taken a few steps toward the stairwell when all hell broke loose. An alarm siren split the air, and a strobe light started pulsing.

"What the..."

"This is a fire drill," a voice said overhead. "All personnel evacuate to the designated assembly point for their sector."

"I don't fricking believe it. A fire drill? Now?" She clasped a hand over the base of her skull, closed her eyes, and delved deep into the data-stream, searching for a way to deactivate the fire drill. Then a thought struck her. *Maybe this could help me. Everyone in this sector will be cleared out for at least ten to fifteen minutes.* Luca came back to the here and now, determined to push on, only for the elevator doors to open again and the same IT guy to step out.

"Hey, you gotta leave. It's a fire drill, come on." He beckoned frantically with one arm, urging her to follow him.

Luca couldn't believe it. What was it going to take to get rid of him? "Yeah, sure. You go ahead, I'll follow in a minute."

"We have to go now. They get very upset if people lag behind. Just letting you know, since you're new here."

"Thanks, but, eh...I gotta take a pee first."

"What? Now?"

"When you gotta go, you gotta go." Luca gave an apologetic shrug. "You go, I don't want you getting into trouble on my account. I'll be up as soon as possible."

For a brief moment she thought he might argue with her again, but he had the good sense to know when he wasn't wanted. So he just nodded. "Uh, okay." And headed back into the elevator.

Luca quickly used her key card to duck into a store room and waited a few minutes for the sector to be cleared. Finally, she made her way down the stairs to the data-vault level.

The area was deserted. She worked her way between tall server racks, then kneeled and removed one of the floor panels that gave access to the mass of cabling that lay underneath. She hid the antimatter device under a particularly dense knot of cables and armed it. "Athena?" she said via her neural-lace. "Armed. Do you have control?"

"Affirmative," came the reply.

"Good. Time for me to get outta here."

Luca began making her way back to the elevator. With most, if not all, of the facility's staff now huddled around various evacuation points outside the complex, presumably cursing the fire drill as they froze in subzero temperatures, Luca met no one on her way to the antenna block, not even IT guy, whom she half expected to jump out at her from a doorway and berate her for not evacuating like the rest of the staff. But she didn't, and she made it back without incident.

A few minutes later, she was wrapped up again in her arctic clothing and making her way along the side of the valley. Two hours after that, she was back on board the transport preparing for takeoff.

She opened a comms channel to Athena. "It's done," she said. "Tell me you still have control."

"Yes, Luca. All systems inside the facility are under my control and the data harvesting is continuing."

"Good, good." Luca breathed a sigh of relief. "And you're not to trigger anything until I say so."

"Of course, as agreed."

"Oh, and make sure Dr. Rayman receives a copy of the data as soon as you've completed the harvesting. She's promised to keep it under wraps until we're ready to release to the wider world."

"Yes, I will ensure she gets a copy. Am I to assume that you are still going ahead with the rest of your plan?"

"Absolutely. Assuming Daedalus is still in orbit?"

"It is. The VanHeilding Corporation are being very cautious about approaching it. I suspect they think it is booby-trapped."

Luca let out a long, slow breath as the transport rose up off the frozen tundra and began banking west out over Baffin Bay.

"This isn't over yet, Athena," she said after a while. "I want to be there when Fredrick VanHeilding watches the destruction of his empire, just so he fully understands who's responsible for his downfall."

"Very well, this is your choice to make. But should you fail in your mission, then the plan will still be activated. The facility will be destroyed and the data released."

"I won't fail, Athena. You can bet on that."

Luca felt the craft pick up speed before dropping down to cruise low over the icy sea.

"Just so you know," Athena continued, "there have been some interesting developments occurring in that region of the solar system. You may remember the QI core that was stolen a while back. It has now resurfaced and is in the hands of a group that is opposed to the takeover by both the VanHeilding and Xiang Zu corporations. This group is suspected to be joining forces with several others that are coalescing around Elektra in the asteroid belt."

"Well, good luck to them. If you're trying to get me to help them, then forget it. I'm not deviating from my mission, not for any reason."

"I understand. But it transpires that the leader of this group, one Dakota Baird, is an old associate of your mother's. He has reached out to her for help."

The craft began to accelerate faster as it headed toward the Davis Strait. "And how did that go down?"

"Your mother, being the proactive person that she is, has orchestrated a mission to rendezvous with this group and attempt to secure the QI core. As I speak, a ship has just left Mars with Miranda, Scott, and Cyrus, along with a cohort of Martian military and some technical people."

"I know what you're trying to do, Athena—lure me into helping them. But it won't work, it's just a distraction. They're more than capable of looking after themselves. I'm not going to be deviated from my objective."

"Very well, just letting you know."

"Okay, thanks for bringing me up to speed. But now, if you don't mind, I'm utterly drained after that ordeal, so I'll sign off." Luca flicked off the comms channel, removed the neural-lace from the base of her skull, and promptly fell asleep.

13

NEWCOMERS

The Martian ship may have been experimental and high-tech, but it was damn slow. Miranda wondered if the budget had run out by the time they got to fitting out the business end of the craft. They'd left Mars thirty-nine sols ago with five trained military and two techs that supposedly knew their way around a QI core. So far, the journey had been tedious and dull apart from regular updates on how the conflict was playing out in the Belt. Mostly this involved a steady build-up around Elektra, with the odd skirmish here and there. Nobody was making any decisive moves just yet.

As for Luca, she had apparently left Earth orbit some time ago and was powering her way back out to the Belt, again. But as usual, any attempt made by either her or Scott to contact was met with stony silence. Even Aria was being vague as to what

Luca had been doing on Earth, saying no more than she went to visit Athena. However, she had also visited Steph, that much Miranda found out from the doctor herself. But she suspected that even she was not telling the full story.

Now, Luca was charging across the solar system in the same stolen ship, presumably with plans of taking on Fredrick VanHeilding at New World One. *Well, good for her,* she thought. *I hope she sticks it to him.*

This, of course, did not help Miranda or anyone on this ship with their current mission. At best it might distract the Xiang Zu Corporation. But they may also see Luca's actions as yet another opportunity to grab more power; it could embolden them to push for a quick resolution to the conflict out here. That is, of course, if they were actually aware of Luca's power, and her singular desire to take down the VanHeilding patriarch.

Scott's voice popped in her earpiece comm. "Miranda."

"Yeah, what is it?" She was down in the armory checking out some of the equipment that the Martians had supplied them with.

"Just received an encrypted message from our pirate friend with a set of coordinates for a rendezvous."

"About time. I was beginning to think he had disappeared and we would never hear from him again. Elektra, I presume?"

"Actually, no. It looks like an old spaceport out in the Berbericia sector."

Miranda considered this for a moment. "Can't say I know much about that area."

"I do. I was at that spaceport, long time ago, collecting

processed ore for the New World One build. It used to be a big, busy port, but most of that area of the asteroid belt was mined out long ago. By the time I was there the place was very rundown, ready to be decommissioned."

"Sounds like the perfect place for a smuggler's hideout."

"If it's the same place I'm thinking of, then it's a fairly long way from Elektra. We could be exposed, and it might be hard to defend if we're attacked."

"Maybe so, Scott. But it looks like that's where we're going. Can you send a reply to confirm?"

"Already done."

Cyrus was not happy. Any inter-ship communications, encrypted or not, could be intercepted. Anyone out there snooping could triangulate its source, even if they couldn't decipher the message.

"We've no choice, Cyrus." Miranda was adamant. "How else are we know where to go? Anyway, I thought this ship is node-runner proof."

"It is. It can't he hacked like the Perception was on the way to Mars. But comms is like leaving a scent, a trail to follow."

They had assembled on the bridge along with the Martian military captain, Ed Rickmann, and the two techs. On the central holo-table a 3D projection of the old spaceport blossomed out from its surface. It was a gnarled mess of docking platforms, storage bunkers, workshop bays, all radiating out from a semi-derelict central core of utility structures, topped off with a sizable artificial gravity torus—now completely stationary relative to the rest of the structure. Jutting out from the central core via flimsy gantries were what looked like a squat power station and an improbable collection of dish antennae. There were no navigation beacons, no lights, nothing to indicate that this was anything other than a derelict hulk.

"Doesn't look very inviting," Miranda said as she studied the image.

"Picking up some thermal activity," said one of the techs, his eyes focused on a data screen. "Looks like they've got power, and there's definite human activity within the central structure."

"See any ship?" asked Scott.

"Not so far," the tech replied.

"There's plenty of old workshop bays where they could keep a small ship hidden and out of the way." Captain Rickmann pointed in the general direction of the spaceport.

"It would be really useful if we could communicate," Scott said, glancing over at Cyrus.

"We don't need to," said Miranda. "We're here now, so I suggest we give it a quick flyby then take the shuttle and bring it in somewhere close to the central structure." She turned to Rickmann. "What do you think?"

The captain screwed his mouth up. "Let's do the flyby first, and see. Hopefully they'll know it's us and won't start taking potshots."

. . .

The ship began a slow circumnavigation of the derelict spaceport at a safe distance, scanning for any more signs of activity.

"There," said Scott, pointing at the image on the ship's main monitor. "Navigation lights."

They were now on the opposite side of the spaceport, and high up on the central structure was a wide docking platform with two navigation beacons flashing on either side.

"That's where they want us to enter," said Miranda, moving closer to the monitor to get a better look.

"Okay, time to suit up," snapped Rickmann. "We'll take the shuttle in close, drop it down on that platform, but keep it ready to lift off again just in case things get hairy."

A few minutes later, Miranda, Scott, and Cyrus were exiting the shuttle and clamping their mag-boots onto the metal surface of the landing platform. Ahead of them, Captain Rickmann and two other Martian military were cauticusly moving toward the airlock door. It hissed open and out came three scruffy looking crew. Their EVA suits were a patchwork of mismatched spare parts. One stepped forward and beckoned for them to enter the airlock.

"Is that him?" Scott asked across the general comm channel.

"Let's find out," said Miranda as she worked her way forward and approached the motley crew. When she got within a meter, she recognized the face of Dakota Baird. He gave her a big, toothy smile accompanied by a wave of his hand. He then pointed at his helmet and signaled that he couldn't communicate.

Miranda signaled that she understood.

"Have we found our man?" Scott asked over their own comm network.

"Yep, that's him. I'd recognize that scumbag anywhere."

Dakota now signaled to follow him into the cargo airlock.

They piled in, let it cycle through its compression routine, and exited into a surprisingly bright, and relatively tidy, former cargo hold. Helmets were removed. Now they could talk.

"Miranda." Dakota's voice was deep and sonorous. "I see the years have been kind to you. You're as radiant as ever." He gestured expansively.

"Cut the crap, Dakota. We've just spent forty-five sols of the most tedious space travel ever experienced, so you better not be bullshitting us about this QI core."

Dakota's face took on a hurt look. "Ah...down to business. Another part of you that hasn't changed with age. Very well, let's dispense with the pleasantries and get on with the main event. This way, follow me." He nodded to his comrades and began working his way along the cargo-hold walkway. Miranda noticed several more of Dakota's crew float out from the shadows, like the ghosts of long-departed mercenaries, and follow along beside them. Most had a hungry, desperate look about them. They all carried plasma pistols and no doubt an assortment of other concealed weapons.

"Hungry looking lot," Scott whispered.

"Yeah, not to be messed with. But still, they'd probably put up a good fight if they had to."

They didn't go far. The QI core had been stashed in an adjoining cargo hold that looked like it was also being used as the crew's living space. Tethered to the walls were a wide assortment of sleeping nets, some with crew still in them, although they were all now wide awake and focused on the newcomers.

"Here it is." Dakota swept an arm toward a sizable, hi-tech container around three meters square. "The most sought-after object in the system."

Cyrus approached and began to examine the crate.

"This better work," Miranda heard someone say from the edge of the group, which now seemed to comprise the entirety of Dakota's crew. They gathered around, watching with eager anticipation as Cyrus commenced his inspection—joined now by herself and Scott.

"Is it the real deal?" Miranda asked.

"I'll tell you in a minute, as soon as I can get this open." Cyrus fiddled with an access panel on the side of the container. He tapped it a few times and the screen illuminated. This elicited a low murmur from the assembled crew, who were inching ever closer to the action.

"This should be it." Cyrus tapped a code onto the screen.

The container gave a slight hiss as it split around the edges and the sides began to slowly hinge open. A faint cloud of vapor escaped and floated motionless in the still air, partially obscuring the contents of the crate. Cyrus leaned in and began waving it away to reveal a squat cylindrical object, which Miranda instantly recognized as the stolen QI core.

The assembled crew were now bunched together, bobbing

and maneuvering to get a better view of this mystical object. It was a moment of awe for them, a moment where the myth of the quantum intelligence had been made a little more real.

Cyrus moved over to the second crate with the superluminal comms unit, opened it, and gave it a quick check. He finally nodded his approval. "I need to run a few tests, but first impressions look good. I think we have a functioning core."

"Good," Dakota announced. "When can we get it online, get it operational?"

"Woah, not so fast." Cyrus looked over at him. "We've got a lot to do. This is just a core, designed to be plugged into an existing infrastructure that was built for it on New World One. We're gonna need a whole lot of work before this baby can do its thing."

This seemed to come as a major surprise to the crew.

"That's not what you told us, Dakota."

"Yeah, you said it just needed to be switched on."

Dakota raised a hand to quiet down the rabble, and turned back to Cyrus. "So, what do you need, and how long is it going to take?"

Cyrus stepped down from the edge of the crate. "We'll need power, and lots of it. We'll also need a decent comms link, one that can jack-in to the grid, with plenty of bandwidth."

"How long?"

Cyrus shrugged. "As long as it takes to put that together."

"Aeon. Brooker," Dakota called out to the crew.

"Here, boss." A thin, older-looking guy floated into view along with a young woman with a useful-looking plasma pistol clipped to her waist.

"Show the newcomers where the old power and comms are on this tub. Maybe they can get it to work."

"What are you using for energy at the moment?" asked Scott.

"We're routing power from the ship," said Brooker. "It was a quick fix, just to get things up and running."

Cyrus shook his head. "Okay, well, we'd better get started."

14

ONE MORE THING

The VanHeilding frigate, now drafted in to help the Xiang Zu Corporation in its efforts to find the missing QI core and bring the conflict in the region to a close, was proceeding at a steady clip toward Elektra, the quadruple asteroid system. However, the primary asteroid was not the ultimate destination, since this was not permanently populated due to its feeble gravity. Most of what people referred to as Elektra was in fact an archipelago of space stations, spaceports, and factory units that had grown together over the decades to form the second-largest populated habitat in the region.

Elektra, like most second cities, always had a rebellious streak. It had never been one to kowtow to the central Belt authority on Ceres—now relocated to New World One. So in many respects, it was understandable that it should become the focus point for every scumbag, mercenary, low-life, and refugee in the system. They were all gravitating toward it like a meteor storm, all hell-bent on putting up a fight. But soon it would be over and all those anarchists would be whipped into shape, whether they liked it or not.

Cortez Ramirez, the ship's commander, almost felt sorry for them as he gazed out of the wide viewing windows on the tactical deck of the frigate. They were still several Earth-days away from arriving at Elektra but he was in no rush. The primary objective of the ship was currently being conducted by a cohort of node runners operating from a section of the ship specifically engineered for such operations. They were all strapped down, jacked-in to the grid, and busy sniffing out ship movements and comms traffic. Their focus was on anything that might give Cortez a clue as to the whereabouts of the treacherous mercenary Dakota Baird, and ultimately, the location of the lost quantum intelligence core.

"Sir," a voice came through on his internal comms unit.

He tapped the side of his head below the right ear to reply. "Go ahead."

"We may have something. A node runner intercepted a comms signal from an unknown ship bound for Elektra. After some further probing, it was established that the ship is hardened against node-runner attack."

"I see." Cortez stroked the long goatee that sprouted from his chin. "And who might possess such a ship?"

"Most likely, it's Martian."

"Interesting. Do we know who they were communicating with? What was being transmitted?"

"No, the message was quantum-encrypted. It seems to have

come from another ship in the Berbericia sector. But that only came alive on transmission and went dead immediately after, no way to trace it."

"A dead ship, very curious. And where is this Martian ship now?"

"Its course has deviated, taking it away from Elektra, out toward the last known location of the dead ship."

"A Martian ship, a quantum-encrypted signal, all very curious." He wheeled around and brought up a system map on the holo-table. "Send me all the location data you have on that region."

Instantly, the map reoriented itself to show the mystery ship's location and vector, and the estimated source of the initial signal. Cortez zoomed in and brought up a data-sheet on the nearest habitable objects in that sector. One piqued his interest, and he gestured to bring up more visual detail. An old derelict spaceport blossomed out over the holo-table, abandoned a long time ago and as such largely forgotten about.

"Well, well." Cortez stroked his goatee again. "Looks like a good place for a clandestine rendezvous. I think we may have found you, Mr. Baird."

He gestured to bring the data up onto the main bridge monitor for all to see. "Any Xiang Zu ships in that area?" he called over to one of the techs.

The chart zoomed way out from the spaceport and several data points flashed up on the chart, each one representing the location of a ship. "The closest is a transport en route to Elektra. It's approximately two days away from that location."

"Okay, alert them that we may have a possible location for Dakota Baird and his crew, and send them all the details."

"Aye, aye, sir."

"One more thing, sir," the node-runner operator's voice returned in Cortez's internal comms.

"Yes, go ahead."

"There is another vessel...eh, a VanHeilding ship heading toward the Belt."

"So."

"It's Daedalus, the one that was stolen from Sebastian VanHeilding, sir."

Cortez froze. *She's back*, he thought. That thorn in the side of the entire family. "Any guesses on its ultimate destination?" he asked, even though he already knew.

"New World One, sir."

"Okay, I'll alert them. In the meantime, keep tabs on it but under no circumstances are you to probe it. Understood?"

"Yes, sir."

He closed the comms connection. *Goddamnit,* he thought, *why do I have to be the one to inform Fredrick VanHeilding.*

15

XIANG ZU

Over the course of a few days, Cyrus, and the Martian techs that had traveled here with them, worked with Aeon and Brooker to figure out what could be salvaged in the old spaceport and what it would take to restart the reactor. This turned out to involve a convoluted process of kickstarting ignition utilizing the reactor on board Dakota's ship. The only caveat according to Cyrus was that that ship would be out of commission for quite some time. How long, he wouldn't say. It depended on a number of factors that Miranda made no attempt to understand. As far as she was concerned, if Dakota needed to temporarily sacrifice his ship for the cause, then so be it. Needless to say, he wasn't happy, nor were his crew. But they had come this far so there was no backing out now.

Miranda spent the evenings on board the Martian ship, along with the others, rather than get friendly with the locals.

Mostly this was about avoiding a situation with Dakota that wasn't purely discussing operational issues. She still hadn't forgiven him for screwing her over. And she probably never would.

Yet, one evening, circumstances conspired to bring them into contact. Scott and Captain Rickmann were somewhere in the sprawling spaceport along with some of the military team reviewing the setup of defensive positions, just in case their location was discovered before the QI went live, and they somehow came under attack. Cyrus, as usual, was over at the reactor with most of the techs, trying to get it operational.

Miranda found herself on the deserted bridge of the Martian ship. She had been surveying some data on Elektra when a comms came in from Dakota requesting urgent supplies of water. Some accident had apparently occurred to drastically diminish their current supplies. Miranda's initial reaction was to ignore it, but there was a genuine tone in his voice.

He can wait until morning, she thought. Then again, he did sound desperate, and it wouldn't put her out too much to do it now.

She gave a sigh and tapped the comms channel. "Miranda here, what's the problem?"

"Ah...Miranda, thanks. Eh...our water supply has somehow become contaminated. It's a bit of a long story, but the thing is, it's not going to go down very well with the rest of the crew when they come back off duty. They're giving me enough guff already about sacrificing the ship's reactor. I'm trying to avoid pissing them off even more."

"The trials and tribulations of command, Dakota. No one thanks you for anything."

"Tell me about it."

"Okay, I'll send you over some from our stores. Hopefully that should fend off an insurrection."

"Thanks."

A few moments later, Miranda was floating into the cargo airlock of the spaceport pushing a bulk container with a thousand liters of H2O. Dakota was waiting on the other side and was clearly surprised to find her doing the delivery by herself. She flipped her visor open. "Here you go. Hope this sorts your command crisis out."

He grasped a handle on the container. "I really appreciate this, but you didn't have to come yourself, you could have sent a minion."

"There's nobody else on board to do it, nobody that's awake that is, and...well, I think you and I need to clear the air. We've been tiptoeing around each other for the last few days. Scott's convinced we had an affair."

Dakota raised an eyebrow. "Really? Well, I'm open to persuasion." He grinned.

"Cut the crap, Dakota. I'm being serious here."

He raised a hand. "My apologies." He lowered his head like he was considering how to respond. "Look, I really appreciate you taking my message seriously and responding to it. I'll admit it was a long shot, considering all that happened."

"You knew that any mention of a QI core was going to get me involved, no matter our past."

"It's what I gambled on. And, well...what happened in the past is best left there. What more is there to say?" He gave a shrug.

"Perhaps," Miranda agreed, her voice conciliatory. "But what I'd like to know is why you did it. Why did you steal from me? You knew what would happen."

Dakota took a deep breath. "Look, I know you'll think this is bullshit, but the truth is it wasn't actually me that did the job on you."

Miranda raised her eyebrows. "Part of the cargo we were transporting for Sicon Industries went for a walk, on your watch." She shook her head. "You have no idea what hell I went through after that. It nearly ruined my security business. Who's going to contract a company to keep things safe, if they can't actually do what they say?"

Dakota raised a hand. "I know, I know, but you were very quick to pin it on me."

Miranda could feel the anger rising before she stopped herself. What would be the point? After all, it was she who wanted to keep things on a professional level. "Someone had to take the fall, Dakota."

They were silent for a while as they pushed the container into an area of the spaceport they were using as a makeshift galley.

"It was Johansson and his crew that did it," Dakota eventually said. "I found out a few months after."

"Johansson? But he had left my crew at least a month before the stuff went missing."

"Exactly, but he still knew the procedures, what contracts we had on, all that. To his credit, he planned well, including having me take the fall."

"That slimy bastard." She shook her head. "I should have known." She looked over at Dakota, who was strapping down the container. "You're not spinning me a line of bullshit on this?"

Dakota shrugged. "Look, if I did it, I'd say so. What does it matter now anyway?" He gestured toward the cargo bay with the QI core.

Miranda considered this. He had a point, and she hated to admit it. That was all in the past. Now they had bigger problems on their hands.

"So now you've gone all freedom fighter," said Miranda as she watched him connect a water line to the container. "How did that happen?"

"Believe it or not, it was during a card game." He looked over and gave her a wry smile.

"What, don't tell me. This is all because you lost a bet?"

"Ha...no, nothing like that. We were holed up over at the Dillon Waystation, and I overheard some refugees from Eugina. They were on their way to Elektra to join the resistance and were hunting for information on the stolen QI. Strange as it may seem, but up until then I hadn't given any thought to what we were carrying in our cargo hold. A job's a job, and all that. Then...well, something kinda opened up in my head, you know. Call it an epiphany, a sudden realization that my life, with all the ducking and diving, was just so much bullshit. And at that moment I felt a need to do something with more...meaning, I suppose. Something that felt...right."

Miranda cocked her head at him. "This better not be another line of crap, Dakota. Because I'm almost beginning to like the new you."

His face grew serious. "No. No crap. The thing is, I got family on Elektra, a brother, married with kids. He's just an ordinary guy, nothing special. Yet he's chosen to throw his lot in with the resistance, stand up and fight for what he believes. And we're talking about a guy who doesn't know one end of a plasma weapon from the other." Dakota lowered his head and gave a shrug. "At the end of the day, I think it was him that made me think about what matters."

"And what's that?"

"People, Miranda. People not getting crapped on by those who just don't give a damn."

Miranda's comm pinged. She held a hand up to Dakota to let him know, and cupped the other over one ear as she responded to the comms. "Yeah, go ahead."

"Where are you?" It was Scott. He was still on the station going over defenses with the captain.

"I'm on the station. Dakota had a H2O crisis so I brought some over. Why? What's the problem?"

"Operations just pinged a ship approaching us, at speed. It could be trouble. Meet us at the cargo airlock. We're heading back to the ship."

"Will do." She turned back to Dakota. "There's trouble heading our way, I gotta get back to the ship."

"Trouble?"

"An unknown ship, coming in fast. You'd better start manning the barricades, just in case."

Miranda deactivated her mag-boots and propelled herself toward the airlock door. Scott, Rickmann, and several of the crew were already there when she arrived. They bundled themselves in and waited while the airlock cycled through the decompression routine. When they stepped out onto the platform, the autonomous shuttle was already opening its side doors and getting ready to take them over to the ship, which was parked in a stationary position relative to the spaceport, around five hundred meters away.

But before anyone had taken another step, out from the blackness of space an incandescent ball of plasma hurtled toward them. It was so fast that nobody had time to react before it slammed into the ship. The blast hit the starboard engine bay and enveloped it in a blinding burst of high-energy chaos. The bay shattered in a cloud of exploding gases, sending chunks of metal in all directions.

"Quick, back inside," Rickmann shouted out. "Before we get hit by debris."

Miranda scrambled backward into the airlock, but just before the doors closed, she watched the shuttle get slammed by the oncoming debris field. It bucked and spun out of control off the platform.

"It's been hit," someone shouted, just as the doors finally shut. They could feel the *thump, thump* of chunks of broken ship slamming against the outer door as the airlock cycled through its compression routine.

Rickmann began shouting commands into his comm. "Get those plasma cannon into action, I want firepower. And get a location on that ship."

They made their way to where the QI core had been stored. An operations room had been set up there over the last few days, more by convenience than by design. A tech operated a bank of monitors, feverishly working through multiple feeds trying to get a lock on the attackers. Dakota was also there, shouting instructions to the crew to take up defensive positions.

"Got it, Captain," the tech called out.

"Why aren't our cannon firing?" Rickmann demanded. "What's the goddamn holdup?"

"Eh...we have a power problem," said the tech, a little sheepishly. But before anyone could respond, a second blast hit the reactor building.

"Cyrus, where the hell is Cyrus?" Miranda looked anxiously at Scott, as the engineer was not responding to her comms.

"It's okay, he's out of there." Scott had no sooner finished the sentence when Cyrus and his team burst in.

"We've a power problem," Captain Rickmann shouted over to him as he entered. "We've no plasma cannon, we can't fire back."

"We've got a limited energy supply, they just need to charge, give it a few more seconds."

"Ship status?" Rickmann call out to the tech.

"Still no response, sir. They're dead in the water."

"Keep trying. There has to be someone still alive on it."

Miranda, like many of the others in the operations room, had been focusing her attention on the monitor feeds. Scenes of chaos unfolded as a third blast hit the docking port superstructure, sending more super-heated shrapnel in all directions and shredding even more sections of the spaceport.

"They're trying to blast us into oblivion," she murmured, just as another blast hit the crippled ship again, this time opening a wide hole in its underbelly. She shook her head. "The ship's gone. No way to salvage that."

Finally, the defensive cannon had reached max power and began firing. Three plasma blasts streaked across the open space toward the attacking ship. Two sailed past harmlessly, but a third hit the nose of the ship, encasing it, for a brief second, in a mesh of high-intensity plasma. But the ship seemed undamaged.

"Keep firing, keep firing," the captain shouted.

But something must have hit home, as the ship slowed, then began to bank away.

"It's changing course, sir."

Another plasma blast streaked across its bow as a second struck the forward undercarriage. Again, the ship seemed undamaged, but it continued its maneuver and then began to retreat.

"Moving away, sir. I think it's backing off."

There was an audible sigh of relief from the assembled crew in the operations room. They would live to fight another day. They had beaten off the attack, for now. But their location was known; there would be another attack soon, probably with more ships, probably one they couldn't fight off.

. . .

"How the hell did they find us?" Dakota gestured at the monitors in the operations room. It was some time later, and full assessment of the damage was still in progress.

"Comms. Has to be that," said Cyrus. "It's the only weak point with the ship. They must have been sifting through communication traffic in this sector."

"Maybe they have node runners," Scott considered.

"That was a Xiang Zu ship. Only VanHeilding uses node runners." Miranda shook her head.

"Then perhaps VanHeilding sees this rogue QI as a top priority, so it donates a team to help them seek it out," Scott continued.

"What the heck is a node runner?" Dakota looked confused.

Miranda rattled off a quick definition. "Genetically enhanced humans with the ability to jack-in to the grid and manipulate the data-stream through thought alone."

"Jesus, are you serious? They can actually do that?" Dakota's eyebrows rose halfway up his forehead.

"Yep. They can take over almost any system." Miranda gestured in the vague direction of the crippled ship. "That ship we came here in has been hardened against a node-runner attack. That's the reason we can't control it remotely, the reason it doesn't have an AI. But as Cyrus said, the only weak point is comms."

Dakota shook his head. Clearly he was having difficulty comprehending this revelation.

. . .

Over the next hour they set about assessing the damage to the spaceport, and more importantly, to the ship. Eventually, Captain Rickmann decided to address everyone and bring them up to speed.

"Okay, listen up." Rickmann faced them holding a slate, which he started reading from. "Still no response from the ship and no way to remotely interrogate it to assess damage other than visually. Starboard engine is gone, we presume the port engine is too. Undercarriage is nonexistent, so we're assuming all internal atmosphere has been expelled. It's also slowly drifting away from us." He glanced up from the slate for a second. "That's probably better than moving toward us, with the potential to smash into the station."

"And the shuttle?" Miranda asked.

He shook his head. "Dead, major structural damage. And drifting away from us at a rate of seven-point-two kilometers per hour."

"What about my ship?" Dakota asked. "It's still in the maintenance hangar."

"Fortunately, it seems your ship has suffered no damage. So we still have that as a life raft."

"Well then, let's get the hell outta here and head for Elektra." Aeon had joined the group, hovering close to Dakota, along with several others of his crew.

"That's five, maybe six days away," said Scott. "How far do you think we'll get before we're blasted into vapor by Xiang Zu?"

"We could make it," Aeon said, a little feebly.

"There's a ship out there just waiting." Miranda pointed in

the general direction of the attack. "As soon as we leave it will be after us, and judging by the damage it did so far, I don't think your ship will be any match for it."

"So, we just sit here and let them gather their forces and attack us again?" Aeon suggested.

"Well, I'd rather go down fighting than get vaporized cowering inside a ship." Angus looked to Dakota, then to the others in the crew.

"Yeah, me too," said Tamires. "Let's take a few of the bastards down with us."

"We would have a chance if we could just get the QI activated," said Scott, and all eyes turned to Cyrus.

"Eh...the antenna array is completely destroyed, and the reactor building is damaged." Cyrus screwed his mouth up and shook his head. "It's simply not possible, with the limited time we have. That ship will be back soon, probably with a load of its buddies."

"It doesn't need to connect to the wider grid," Scott considered. "If we could get it powered up and simply operating on the local broadcast radius of the spaceport, that could be enough for it to disable any ship that comes within attacking range."

Again, Cyrus screwed his mouth up and thought about this for a moment. "Well, if we're all agreed that we're not going to try and make a run for Elektra, then I suppose we could somehow try and scrounge enough power to get it partially activated."

"What about the ship's reactor? Maybe it survived. Could we use that?" All eyes turned to the tech.

Cyrus nodded slowly. "Possible, but how? It's floating away from us."

"We use my ship," said Dakota. "I can get it close enough to get someone over to the wreck. Then we can find out what's salvageable."

There was silence in the room for a moment as each of them started coming to terms with what their options were. Make a run for Elektra and try and beat the odds of being blown to bits by a fleet of Xiang Zu ships. Or hunker down in the spaceport and fight it out to the bitter end.

"Is it possible to bring that ship in and dock it to the spaceport?" said Miranda.

"Are you crazy," said Rickmann. "There was a reason we didn't do this when we arrived."

"That was so we didn't damage the ship. But we're way past that now." She turned to Dakota. "Could you do it, using your ship as a tug?"

"I could do it," Scott jumped in. "That's what I was doing for several years, shifting ore barges around, docking, undocking. If your ship has reasonable reaction control then I'm pretty sure I could do it."

They looked at each other for a moment.

"Okay," Miranda finally announced. "We get it back and physically docked. That way we can work faster."

Rickmann swung around to face Miranda. "How do you know the reactor on that ship isn't about to go critical? Because if it does, it'll take this entire station with it." He gestured wildly with his arms.

"If it is, then we're screwed anyway," Cyrus intervened.

"Dakota, want to give it a go?" Scott looked over at the mercenary.

He opened his hands in a gesture. "If you think you can do it, then my ship is yours."

"Cyrus, you're coming with me, and you too Miranda." Scott pointed at both of them in turn. "We'll need some people suited up and on rope duty."

"Ropes?" Miranda looked confused.

"We're docking a dead ship. Trust me, we'll be doing this the old-school, time-honored way."

16

GODFORSAKEN UNIVERSE

Scott took the smuggler's ship out to where the Martian craft drifted. Several of Dakota's crew then went EVA and attached a number of tethers to the hull. As soon as they were clear, Scott gently pushed the dead ship with the blunt nose of Dakota's ship toward the spaceport. Then the tricky part came. He reversed thrust to take up the slack on the tethers and slow it down. All the time he worked with the small, omnidirectional gas thrusters, which made for precise but painfully slow progress.

At one point, very close to the docking truss, he lost control and the rear end of the ship swung out wildly, putting an enormous strain on the tethers. This sent Miranda and the others, who were suited up and waiting on the truss to attach ropes to the hull and secure it in place, all scrambling for safety. But the tethers held, Scott regained control, and a short time later they had it secured to the dock. An umbilical was then connected to the auxiliary docking port on the Martian ship. They pressurized the access tunnel along the dock, and finally they could enter the ship and do a full damage inspection. This still required them to be in EVA suits when passing through the airlock from the docking tunnel, but at least now they could work with speed. Miranda was first on board along with Cyrus, Rickmann, and two techs. They were met with a lot of debris floating in the interior, including the body of one of the crew who had been on board and sleeping at the time of the attack.

They made their way to the bridge and Cyrus began checking out the systems. He plugged in a portable diagnostics terminal, tapped a few commands, and the bridge flickered to life with a multitude of illuminated displays, audible alerts, and flashing warnings.

"I take it the reactor is still functioning, then?" said Miranda.

"This is just from auxiliary power, but it's looking promising." He swiveled his head to look back at her and the captain. "I think we're in luck."

Rickmann glanced around at the floating detritus. "I wouldn't call this luck."

Over the next few hours, Cyrus and the tech team worked to route power from the ship, utilizing the existing cabling that ran the length of the docking truss, into the operations room where the QI core was located.

Scott brought Dakota's ship back into the maintenance hangar, which they reckoned was the safest place to put it. This was an enclosed space, so the ship couldn't be seen, and hopefully couldn't be targeted. It was probably the reason it had survived the first attack. Dakota and his crew then busied themselves removing the exterior plasma cannon and relocating it to a location on the spaceport that needed more coverage.

Miranda and Captain Rickmann worked on a defensive plan, which involved several fallback levels. The first line of defense were the plasma cannons, of which they had four, including the one from Dakota's ship. They considered trying to get the one on the Martian ship operational, but it was destroyed when the undercarriage was hit.

If this first line was breached and Xiang Zu tried to infiltrate the actual spaceport, then it would be down to small weapons fighting, and pulling back into the operations room, where they would make a last stand. Already, most of the access points were being welded shut and barricades and obstacles placed along the corridors to slow any advance and provide cover for a retreat. They just had to hold out and hope that Cyrus could do the impossible, and get the QI operational.

"Here you go, thought you might be hungry." Scott floated over to Miranda and offered her a ration pouch.

Miranda wiped her hands on her jacket and reached out. "Thanks, I'm starving." She tore the cap off and took a mouthful of the thick glucose and protein goo. "How's Cyrus doing?"

"Stressed. Best not go near him at the moment."

"Does he think it can be done, get the QI operational?"

Scott cocked his head. "I'll be honest, I think it's fifty-fifty."

"Then we're screwed, aren't we?"

"We've been in tighter spots." He grinned. "We'll find a way."

They were quiet for a time, both eating, both looking around at the feverish preparations going on all around them.

"I wonder where Luca is now?" Miranda said between mouthfuls of food. "Did she make it to New World One?"

"Yeah, she's probably fighting her own battles as we speak."

"I hope she has better odds than we have."

"Quiet! Quiet!"

They looked over at the central hub to see Captain Rickmann waving a hand to quiet everybody down. He then looked back at the bank of monitors and listened to something the tech was saying. He relayed the message.

"They're back...two ships... No, make that three...closing in fast...within range in seven minutes."

Everybody directly involved in the defense scrambled to their stations.

Scott looked back at Miranda. "Time to get the game face on."

The first barrage came a little after the seven-minute mark. All three ships fired multiple plasma blasts, not all of which struck home as the attacking craft were still some distance out. Of the blasts that found their target, damage was marginal, yet the entire spaceport shook with the impacts.

But this time they were ready. Four exterior-mounted plasma cannon let rip, pounding out a barrage of high-energy plasma, all directed at the lead ship. Most went wide of the mark, sailing harmlessly off into the void. One grazed the underbelly of the ship, effecting minimal damage. But one slammed directly into its bow. A cheer went up in the operations room where many were now gathered, watching events play out on the monitors.

But the ships kept advancing, retargeted their weapons on the spaceport's gun emplacements. One was knocked out completely, and one lost targeting capability, but only momentarily.

"Miranda." Scott came up beside her at the tech station. "Cyrus has a problem, needs our help." He jerked his head over at the engineer, who seemed to be tracking a bunch of thick cables that hung across the cargo bay.

"What's the problem?"

"There's a drop-off in power from the ship's reactor. It happened just after the first barrage. He thinks it's a high-impedance short."

"I've got no idea what that means," Miranda replied. "Give it to me in English."

"We need to check the cables all the way back to the ship. They might have gotten twisted up, or some debris could have lodged in one of them."

Miranda sighed. "Okay, let's get to it."

They moved off and down to the lower dock level through an access tunnel, following the thick, armored cable that ran as far as an industrial junction box. This is where it was connected to the exterior dock cabling. They passed through a small maintenance airlock and out onto the underside of the main docking truss. This was a wide metal superstructure crisscrossed with beams and support joists.

"This is it." Scott pointed at a wide line of ducting that ran the entire length of the dock. Flashes of plasma fire lit up the superstructure as they followed the cabling, looking for damage.

"There!" Scott shouted. "Up ahead."

The overhead docking platform had taken a hit, creating a tangled web of bent and broken metal.

"This looks bad," said Miranda as she tried to make sense of the mess.

Scott moved around, inspecting it from different sides. "All the wiring is still intact, but it's been skewered by this broken joist. That's probably what's causing the short. We just need to pull it out. Come on, give me a hand."

But Miranda hesitated for a beat as she looked out toward the attacking ships. They had stopped firing. Odd.

"What is it?" Scott asked, looking up at her.

Miranda didn't reply immediately; she was transfixed by a series of glistening specks that spewed out from one of the ships. "Scott, look. Do you see what I see?"

Scott glanced up at the ships and studied the specks growing in size as they sped toward them. "I could be wrong," he said, "but that looks suspiciously like a swarm of battle-droids—heading our way."

Miranda grabbed his arm. "We'd better get a move on."

They worked their way as fast as they could around to

where the broken joist protruded from the cabling duct. Scott delicately touched the metal beam protruding from the cable duct, testing if it was live. Yet, even if it was, the thick gloves on his EVA suit should be enough to insulate him. Confident he wasn't going to get zapped, Scott began wrestling with the joist. "That's wedged in tight. Going to need your help with this."

Miranda grabbed the joist and the two of them began working it slowly up and out. With one last effort, they freed the joist and let it float away.

"Cyrus, tell me you've got power back." They began working their way back as Scott checked in with the engineer. He gave Miranda the thumbs-up. "Looks like that was the problem."

"Well, we've got a few more problems heading our way." Miranda glanced up at the swarm. The exterior defense cannon were firing wildly, desperately trying to pick off the battle-droids before they arrived. But most were getting through.

Like avatrons, battle-droids were remotely operated, but unlike their more benign brethren, they were semi-autonomous, meaning one operator could control several of these machines at the same time. They were fast, well-armed, ultra-maneuverable, and extremely dangerous—and they were nearly on top of them.

"Move, come on, no time to hang around," Scott urged.

They worked their way back along the central docking truss and were nearly at the maintenance airlock when one landed with a thump on the dock, around two hundred meters away. It immediately let rip with a burst of plasma fire that peppered the area around them.

"Shit." Miranda ducked instinctively and returned fire,

winging the machine and sending it spinning backward for a moment before it regained control.

Scott had the airlock door open and began shouting into his comm. "Get in, quick. You can't fight those things out in the open, Miranda."

The distance between her and the open door was around twenty meters, not far but she didn't have much time, as a second battle-droid landed close beside the first one. She took a chance, kicked off from the dock superstructure into free space, aiming for the door. Two blasts hit the structure where she had just vacated. Her trajectory was slightly off, but Scott reached out and grabbed her wrist, pulling her in through the door and slamming it closed.

"Cyrus!" Miranda shouted into her helmet comm as they exited the airlock and came into the maintenance tunnel. "Give us some good news, because we're about to get hammered."

Before she got a reply, a violent tremor shook the tunnel, sending them bouncing off the walls.

"What the hell was that?" Miranda glanced over at Scott, who was scrambling to get a handhold.

When he finally managed to stabilize himself, he replied, "They must have hit something big."

Miranda looked back at him. "Big like the ship?"

"Cyrus, do you hear me?" Scott called into his comm.

"I hear you." Cyrus's voice sounded deflated.

"Talk to me, can we get that QI activated?"

There was a delay in the response.

"Gone... The ship's gone. They must've hit the reactor in the last barrage. Power is gone. Nothing..." His voice trailed off.

Miranda was about to ask him if there was anything that could be done, but she knew it was pointless. He had done everything he could. They all had. All that was left now was trying to stay alive.

They floated there in silence for a brief moment as the reality of their situation dawned on them. But their moment of reflection didn't last long, as several more blasts could be heard coming from the direction of the airlock they had just passed through. The battle-droids were breaking in. They had to move, no time to waste.

They came to a defensive barricade that had been established outside the entrance to the operations room and where Cyrus had been working on the QI core. Three Martian military crew had taken up a position behind a light plasma cannon. Anything coming down this tunnel would be in for a fight. They were in full EVA suits, ready for the moment when the spaceport finally lost compression, and judging by the intensity of the assault, that wouldn't be long coming. They moved past the barricade and into the operations area. Anxious faces greeted them.

Captain Rickmann beckoned to them from behind a bank of monitors. "We're being hammered," he said with a shake of his head.

Miranda looked at the monitors, at the running battles playing out in and around the access routes to this area of the spaceport. Martian and smuggler, fighting side-by-side, trying to hold back an army of battle-droids.

"I've given the command for everyone to fall back. We'll try and defend the entrances to this area. But if that fails, then we'll get everyone inside, seal up the doors, and make a last stand in here."

Already, fighters were piling back in through the two routes still open. Many were injured, some were dead, all looked worn and haggard.

Dakota was amongst the last to arrive. He came over when he spotted them gathered around the monitors. "Where's the honor in fighting machines? Those things are diabolical, they're mowing us down," he said breathlessly.

Rickmann shook his head again. "All our exterior cannon are down, they could annihilate us with just their ships' firepower, so why are they sending these killing machines?"

"They want the QI," said Cyrus. He had given up on his quest to get the QI core activated, and instead watched the carnage playing out across the spaceport.

"Then we should destroy it, rather than let them have it." Miranda looked over at the engineer.

"Already thought of that." Cyrus showed them a control switch he held in his hand. "I wired the core to go boom. Only problem is when it does, we all go down with it." He held a thumb over the push button to emphasize the point.

The last of the fighters scrambled in and others began welding the doors shut. Captain Rickmann cast them a worried glance. "Don't know how long that's going to hold them."

"Sir," a tech called over, "another ship has just shown up. Small, looks like a luxury cruiser."

"Great," said Scott. "They're selling tickets to the show, now the fat cats are turning up to enjoy their moment of triumph."

"Positions everybody," Rickmann shouted out on general comms. "We take down anything that tries to break in."

Miranda gripped Scott's gloved hand. He looked at her, a little surprised. She turned into him, placed a hand behind his head, and they knocked visors. No words were spoken—they didn't have to.

They broke apart, then took up positions behind one of the many hastily assembled barricades. Cyrus joined them, plasma pistol in one hand, detonator in the other.

It didn't take long for the machines to start cutting through the access doors. First, they glowed red hot, turning to white as the laser cutters began scything through the thick steel. When it had completed its loop around the door, the cut was kicked in, flailing across the cargo-bay space and crashing into the opposite wall. Two battle-droids scrambled through, firing bursts at the defenders along the barricades. The machines were met with a crescendo of return fire. Both droids never made it more than a few meters. But more came, and kept coming.

Miranda grabbed Scott's arm. "We're running out of time." They were being assailed with plasma fire; bodies floated past them. She turned to look at Cyrus, who crouched on the floor with his back to the barricade. Cyrus looked from one to the other, then nodded. He held out a balled fist.

Miranda grabbed it, wrapping her hand around. Scott

followed with his hand. Finally, Dakota floated over and placed his on top. Cyrus again looked from one to the other, flicked the safety cap off the detonator, and his thumb hovered over the button. He took one last look over at the raging battle and noticed something odd.

The battle-droids were shutting down. His thumb hesitated. "Look—the droids, they're deactivating."

Miranda opened her eyes, and sure enough the machines had stopped firing, retracted their weapons' systems, and folded up their four limbs into a kind of fetal position. They were also being bombarded with plasma fire from all sides as the crew took the opportunity to attack them unopposed. Some crew were also beginning to come out from behind cover and moving in for the kill.

"What the..." Miranda looked at Cyrus and grabbed his detonator hand, preventing him from depressing the button. "Hold that thought, Cyrus. Something's up."

The engineer took his thumb away and flicked the safety cover back into position, just as a loud burst of static come over the general comms. "Aghh..." Miranda clasped a hand to the side of her helmet, frantically turning the volume down, as did every other person left alive in operations room.

Then she heard a voice, one she recognized. "Cease firing, cease firing. The droids are no threat now."

The others must have heard this too, as the level of violence directed at the machines dialed down a few notches.

"I said, cease firing. We're going to need those droids."

The firing stopped, to be replaced with a universal sense of confusion by the crew as they all tried to get some understanding of who this voice belonged to.

The main operations console had been shot to bits. Monitors floated cracked and broken around the area; some still had cables attached and so just dangled in place. But some of the equipment began to pop back to life, lights flickering. Cracked screens began displaying scrolling lines of code, comms buzzed and crackled. Everybody began to move closer to the wrecked console to witness this bizarre anomaly.

One screen still intact, dangling on its wire tether, flickered to life and a human face began to form. It was a young woman, head tilted back, eyes half closed with only the whites showing. The group moved in closer to get a better look at this ghostly apparition. Suddenly her eyes snapped open, and the group jolted back a little. She spoke.

"The battle is over, all Xiang Zu ships are disabled. I'm coming on board."

The screen went dark.

"Who, in the name of all that is holy in this godforsaken system, is that?" Dakota spoke for everyone.

"She," said Miranda, clutching Scott's hand, "is our daughter."

17

GAME ON

She had almost left it too late. Another second or two and the outcome might have been vastly different. Nevertheless, a considerable amount of death and destruction had been inflicted by the time she finally did show up.

From the very outset, Luca had been determined not to get involved in the conflict that was brewing out at Elektra. She had other objectives, so this was not her fight. But throughout the initial stage of her journey from Earth to the asteroid belt, Athena had been updating her on the progress of the Martian expedition to recover the stolen QI—notwithstanding the fact that she had blocked all communications with the ship. But no matter what firewall she put on the ship's systems, the QI always found a way to circumvent it.

She knew what it was doing, of course. It was trying to get her involved. Not overtly; QIs rarely came at you head-on. Their methods were more oblique, nudging people and events in the direction they wanted them to take without them really knowing. Yet, by sending her these reports in the manner in which they came, Athena was exhibiting the closest thing a QI could come to outright pleading.

And it had the desired result. She found herself reading them and latching on to the fate of her family and friends. But it wasn't the fact that their mission had located the missing QI that roused Luca from her indifference—it was the presence of node-runner activity that had tipped the balance for her.

She had assumed that they would be on the lookout for her approach to New World One, but this activity was emanating from a VanHeilding ship much farther out. At that range, her ability to interrogate their systems was limited but she did figure out that they had a potential lead on the location of the stolen QI and were passing this information on to any Xiang Zu ships in close proximity.

This prompted Luca to finally break her communications silence and contact Athena. Between them, they analyzed all current data points and concluded that if the Mars mission was indeed heading for that location—an old, semi-derelict spaceport in the Berbericia sector—then it wouldn't be long before Xiang Zu forces encircled them. They would be seriously outgunned, and complete annihilation was a distinct possibility.

Much to the satisfaction of the QI, Athena, Luca instructed the ship's AI to calculate an optimal course to the Berbericia sector. She had the advantage of having a very fast ship, but even with this she wouldn't arrive until after the Xiang Zu forces. She considered that she might be too late already. So, she hacked the ship's operating parameters to push the engines a few percent beyond the recommended safety limit, saving her an extra day—assuming that the ship didn't disintegrate in the process.

And so, for the second time en route to confront Fredrick VanHeilding on New World One, Luca changed course. At least this time she would still be in the same broad region of space, and not going backward.

By the time the ship got to within range of the old spaceport, a raging firefight was already in progress. Three Xiang Zu ships were bombarding the peripheral structure with plasma fire while a contingent of battle-droids tore their way into the central core, presumably where the defenders had decided to hole up. Luca activated her neural-lace and went hunting.

There were no node runners on the Xiang Zu ships, nor anywhere in the vicinity—this was good. It would make life a little easier for her. She reckoned that the VanHeilding Corporation did not trust Xiang Zu with its most potent weapon, preferring instead to offer intelligence-gathering facilities rather than allowing them direct control.

She probed the first ship within range. It was the smallest of the three and so had hung back a little, shielding itself from the fusillade of plasma-cannon fire emanating from the spaceport. Within a few microseconds, Luca had obliterated the ship's firewalls and began manipulating its AI to deactivate all systems excluding life-support. In an instant it lost all motive power, weapons control, and communications. Likewise, she did the same to the next ship in the fleet.

The final ship was where the battle-droids were being operated from, and it took her a few extra microseconds to wrest control from the human operators. With all data comms channels now disabled, the battle-droids defaulted to fail-safe and automatically deactivated themselves.

She then bent her mind to the spaceport and tried to find a data route in. This was much trickier than the ships since most of its comms systems were either disabled or destroyed. But find a way she did, and she sent a broadcast message for them to stop fighting. The battle was over, she was now in control, and she would be paying them a visit momentarily.

Luca brought her ship in as close as she dared to the mangled docking port, instructing it to maintain its position. She put on her EVA suit, and with the help of a thruster pack, exited the ship and flew over to one of the few airlocks on the spaceport that still functioned.

I can't believe you're here, Luca," said her stunned mother.

"We thought you were on the New World," said an equally stunned Scott.

They had met her coming out of the airlock and taken her to their operations room, a cavernous cargo hold, where she was greeted with muted silence by a motley crew of Martian military and scruffy mercenaries. There were dead and injured, being hastily treated and comforted by friends and comrades. Debris floated everywhere, along with the torn and broken carcasses of battle-droids. In the center of the space was the stolen QI core; a multitude of cables and ducting snaked out from the casing to broken and disheveled banks of equipment. Cyrus glanced over from behind this chaos and waved. She waved back and gave a smile, happy to see that he was also still alive.

Atmospheric pressure had been restored to this space, so she flipped open her visor and turned to Miranda and Scott, who were busy explaining who she was to the others. "I've disabled the Xiang Zu ships, but more are coming. Two more to be precise, and they'll be here in less than three hours."

She raised a hand to quiet the barrage of questions being thrown at her. "While that's not a major problem, there's also a well-armed VanHeilding ship monitoring the situation, and if it gets no reply from the Xiang Zu force, it'll start to investigate. They're in a completely different league, as they have a cohort of node runners on board. So you all need to get out of here as soon as possible."

There was a momentary silence as the assembled crew tried to assimilate all this information.

"We take my ship and the QI core and head for Elektra. That's where the fight is." A scruffy looking mercenary gestured at what looked to be his comrades for approval. But the response was muted.

"Your ship is destroyed, Dakota. The hangar was hit with several plasma blasts, the place is a wreck," said Cyrus as he joined the group surrounding Luca.

"So the only way off this spaceport is on your ship, Luca," said Miranda, pointing at her.

"I'm going to New World One. I have a date with destiny, and believe me, you don't want to go that way."

"So we just stay here and wait to be attacked again?" said Dakota. "And can someone please tell me how the hell you did that, disable those ships with not so much as a whisper?" he continued.

Luca considered this a moment, then decided to indulge this question. "You know about node runners, genetically enhanced humans that can jack-in to the grid and manipulate the data-stream?"

There were a few nods, but mostly blank faces.

"I possess such abilities. So it was a relatively simple matter for me to screw with the AI controlling those ships."

"But how...?"

Luca raised a hand. "Enough. I'll talk no more about it. Just accept I can do these things."

"Then come to Elektra, we could use someone with your abilities. We could defeat Xiang Zu, and save a lot of lives in the process," Dakota pleaded.

"No, not my fight. My path leads to New World One and the VanHeilding Corporation."

"But they know you're coming, they're expecting you." Miranda's face took on a concerned look. "They'll have everything they've got armed and ready to take you on. How sure are you of getting past all that?"

"Well, it turns out that this little detour to save all your asses can actually work to my advantage. There's a VanHeilding ship lying in wait for me, but it has one eye on this skirmish. Once it realizes they've lost communications with the Xiang Zu attack fleet, I'm hoping it'll come out here and investigate. That'll divert it and possibly allow me to pass without being noticed."

"I still say the best option is to help us defeat the forces trying to subjugate Elektra. Once we do that, then we can gather our resources and travel together to take on New World One." Dakota spread his hands out, appealing to her.

"I'm not going to Elektra. Like I said, that's your fight. But I will help you get there. You can take my ship, it's fast and very well armed. You can do a serious amount of damage with it."

Dakota's eyes widened. "Seriously? And what about you?"

"I'm going to take one of the Xiang Zu ships. That way I stand a better chance of approaching New World One without being discovered."

There was a pause in the discussions as they each considered Luca's plan.

"What about the QI core?" Cyrus finally asked. "Everything we tried to do still stands. If we can get that up and running, then the war is pretty much over."

"We go with Luca and take it with us," said Scott. "It was designed for the habitat, the support infrastructure is already in place. If we can get inside, then it's possible. And let's face it, Cyrus, you know every nook and cranny in that place. It can be done."

Miranda nodded. "Scott's right. If Luca can get us in, then we have a good shot at finishing this."

Cyrus scratched his chin. "Hmmm...it might be possible." He looked from Luca to Scott to Miranda and gave a shrug. "Okay, let's finish this, once and for all."

18

ANOTHER HORIZON

In saving her parents from death at the hands of a Xiang Zu droid army, Luca now found herself being convinced into helping them get the QI core installed in New World One. Yet, her own objective had always been simple ever since she left Mars in Sebastian VanHeilding's ship, and that was to put an end to Fredrick VanHeilding. But this seemingly clear objective had been building in complexity and audacity as she bent her mind to its execution. Already she had acquired the wherewithal to strike a critical blow to the power of the VanHeilding Corporation, but if this new QI could be made active at the same time, then it would mean that the current fight for control within the solar system would be brought to a close. The growing ambitions of VanHeilding, Xiang Zu, and the other families would be curtailed, and the old ways of constant conflict and strife could be tempered. Couple this with the system-wide release of the VanHeilding genetic data research, then humanity truly had the potential to level up as a civilization.

It was at that moment that she realized the QIs' true intentions and the sheer scale of their vision. *Oh my God,* she thought. *This was their plan all along.* How did she not see it before now?

Then another thought began to form. *Have they been manipulating me into doing this? Am I just another element in their grand equation?* This thought troubled her, as she'd been under the assumption, ever since leaving Mars, that she had been making her own decisions, charting her own course, defining her own destiny. Maybe this was all just an illusion.

But perhaps *manipulation* was too strong a word. The QIs, after all, operated with a vastly more nuanced agenda than simply playing tricks on people to get them to do what they wanted. They operated in a multidimensional space where all, or almost all, possible outcomes that mattered were permutated and extrapolated out along an elongated timeline. With that much prescience, all they really had to do was nudge a little here and there for events to unfold along their preferred preordained path. This was, in effect, how they had managed to maintain balance within the affairs of humanity and prevent it from indulging in the detrimental excesses that had cursed human civilization for millennia.

But they could not foresee everything. Their abilities were limited to the extent of the data points available to them, and with the rise of the node runners, and the loss of the QI on

Ceres, gaps began appearing in this data set. *Have they foreseen this too?* she thought. *They must have*, she concluded. *How could they not.* Yet they would have compensated for this probability, readjusted their equation, added some new elements that would rebalance it.

She had been one of those elements. That time on her twenty-third birthday when Dr. Rayman arrived with a present from Athena, that was the moment when they brought her into their plan. And ever since then they had been adjusting and tweaking their predicted path, a hundred billion times a second for all she knew.

Her own path had been to travel at top speed to confront Fredrick VanHeilding out at New World One. But that path had been tweaked and nudged several times already by Athena and the QI hive-mind. Now she had ended up out here at this broken-down old spaceport, ostensibly to save her folks' asses from ending up as droid fodder. Yet laid out before her were a multitude of fortuitous sidebars. She now had the stolen QI core in her possession, and a Xiang Zu ship, giving her the opportunity to journey to New World One incognito. Not only that, but she also had Cyrus and his intimate knowledge of the habitat, giving her a better option to gain access to its interior. And to top it all, she had a decoy in the form of the smuggler Dakota Baird taking the very ship VanHeilding would be looking for away in the opposite direction, to the asteroid enclave of Elektra. Coincidence? She didn't think so. The QIs had predicted all this. They were helping her achieve her objective—which was ultimately their own objective.

Yet somewhere in the back of her mind, she felt that there was possibly more to the QIs' grand vision than she could truly see. Another horizon beyond the perceived terminus of her current path. Some greater destination still shrouded in mystery, to be revealed to her only when the QIs deemed the time was right.

19

HANDSHAKE

They decanted the twenty or so crew from the smallest of the Xiang Zu ships onto a shuttle using the persuasive power of two battle-droids, which were being controlled by Luca back on the spaceport.

Any operations' room equipment that had not been trashed during the fight had been hastily jerry-rigged together, and got working enough so that Luca could jack-in to the local area data-stream. Along with controlling the shuttle that was ferrying the subdued Xiang Zu crew to one of their other disabled ships, Luca also remotely piloted the newly commandeered ship in closer to the spaceport so they could get the QI core transferred. While she was doing this, she also used its communications systems to scan the local sector to identify any ships in the vicinity that needed to be avoided. But she resisted the temptation to probe the VanHeilding ship in case the node runners sensed her presence in the data-stream.

All this she conducted from a floating position tethered to the salvaged comms equipment via a web of cables. To those who passed her, she seemed to be unconscious, with half-closed eyes rolled back in her head. Many gaped in wonder at this curious individual and her ever-present micro-drone perched beside her. Unbeknownst to them, she could hear their whispers as they passed.

The Martian crew viewed her as a secret weapon. They had some knowledge and understanding of node runners, they had heard the stories, knew how they operated, and what they could do. But mostly they knew how feared they were among the Mars Council. Even their own ship had been hardened against node-runner attack.

But to Dakota Baird's ragtag crew of mercenaries, she was something beyond comprehension. All they had to work with were tall tales spoken in hushed tones of strange, genetically modified creatures with even stranger super powers. Most of these stories were regarded with a large dollop of skepticism, like most stories told by travelers in late-night bars around card tables. Yet, there was enough substance in their telling to create a mystique, even superstition.

Up until now, Luca's true abilities were only known to a select few people—not anymore. Dakota's crew would spread their tales of her to all who would listen on Elektra, and from there they would spread to other worlds. These stories would be embellished and grow with each telling until she would be imagined as some sort of superbeing, one who'd singlehandedly destroyed an entire fleet of battleships with nothing more than a thought. In time, she would be viewed with both awe and fear, perhaps even worshipped as a god. This was not a prospect she relished.

They said their goodbyes as Dakota and his crew powered up Daedalus and charted a course for Elektra. The rest of them boarded the Xiang Zu ship and headed for New World One, a six-day journey. As for the other two ships, they were left immobilized and without communications. All they could do was wait and hope that the VanHeilding ship would come to investigate why all contact had been lost. This was something Luca was betting on.

The ship was slow and unsophisticated, an ex-transport that had been commandeered by the Xiang Zu Corporation in some earlier skirmish with a lesser mining family out in the Belt—like most of their current fleet of ships. But what it lacked in creature comforts it made up for in stealth, able to slip quietly through Belt space without raising any suspicions.

They were two days out from the old spaceport when Luca sensed the VanHeilding ship finally make its move, and as predicted, it headed out to the Berbericia sector to investigate the total communication silence from the Xiang Zu fleet. With that threat passing, she now bent her mind to the challenge of gaining access to New World One.

The bridge on the ship was cramped, with just enough room for around six people, at most. Luca was strapped into one of the cockpit seats, jacked-in to the ship's systems, and scanning local space for activity. They were still way out from the New World One habitat, but close enough for Luca to latch on to one of the perimeter navigation beacons on the edge of its farthest border. With this she had access to all shipping information coming in and out of the vast habitat city. It was busy, with thousands of datapoints, from big industrial transports to light pleasure cruisers, and everything in between. Most of the mid to light craft were being directed in and out of the huge docking port on the aft end of the vast cylinder. The bigger ships were taking up parking positions a little way out from the habitat, and using shuttles to ferry goods and people to and from the dock.

So far no one had paid any attention to them. Luca had masked the ship's identity as a simple goods transport operating under the Xiang Zu insignia. Soon though, she would be getting a handshake from the habitat's traffic control AI and be slotted into a queue. All very normal, all very mundane. Except they wouldn't be landing at the dock; Cyrus had worked out a better way in.

She jacked out of the data-stream and swung her seat around to face the others who had gathered around the small, central holo-table.

Cyrus fiddled with the 3D projection of the vast space-city. "The datacenter is located here, around midway along the first sector of the habitat. That's where we need to get to, that's where the infrastructure to accept the QI core is installed."

"How do we know it's all still there and functioning, and that they haven't ripped it out?" said Rickmann. The Martian captain had initially been reluctant to endorse this high-stakes mission, but in the end, what choice did he and his team really have—stay on the spaceport? Take his chances with Dakota and head for Elektra? None of these were serious options, so with a reluctant shrug he gathered the remains of his crew and boarded the Xiang Zu transport.

"Can you find out?" Scott said, as all eyes turned to Luca.

She shook her head. "As soon as I try to access the hab's data-stream there's a high likelihood that any node runner monitoring the system will sense my intrusion. They would then know I'm here, somewhere close. What I'm saying is, if I try to establish if the QI infrastructure is still functioning, there's a big risk I would just be giving the game away."

"Then we're taking a big risk going in if we don't know for sure," Rickmann fired back.

"We've come this far. We're not turning back now." Miranda cast him a quick glance, inferring that this wasn't open for discussion.

"Once we're in, I can find out for sure," Luca elaborated. "I can also create a diversion or two, just to throw them off the scent and send them heading in the wrong direction. That way you'll have a good chance at getting it up and running."

Scott turned back to the projection over the holo-table. "So what do you reckon is the best way in, Cyrus?"

The engineer gestured at the projection; it zoomed in to a section of the exterior with a cluster of communications dishes and antennae. "There's a maintenance hatch here which should be large enough to accommodate all the QI components."

The projection then morphed into an interior schematic.

"We can take this maintenance tunnel here, which should bring us about halfway. After that it gets too narrow, so at that point we'll need to exit onto the interior surface."

"We're going to be very exposed up there," said Miranda. "Anything we can use as cover?"

"I can commandeer a ground car, have it waiting at that exit point and program it to travel all the way to the closest drop-off area," said Luca.

"Excellent, make sure it's a goods transport, we'll need something big," Scott said as he studied the schematic of the datacenter. "Lot of security around there, lot of people too. So how do we get through all that?"

"We could just break cover and shoot our way in." Miranda gestured at the schematic. "Once inside we hold out until the QI goes live."

"How long does that take, Cyrus?" Scott asked.

The engineer shifted a little and ran a hand over his bald head. "Good question."

"Best guess?" Miranda prompted.

"Assuming that everything still operates as it should, then it's a relatively simple matter of inserting the core. Then it should boot up, access the habitat's data-stream, and seek out a connection to the QI hive-mind via its super-luminal communications system. If all that happens, there will still be a period of time when it synchronizes with the other QIs. How long that takes, I really don't know."

"An hour, a week?" Miranda pushed.

"No, nothing like that." Cyrus shook his head. "But twenty

minutes could be a long time if we're trying to prevent the barbarians from storming the castle."

Luca raised a hand to stop them talking, as her other hand touched her temple. "Handshake with traffic control, they've given us a slot, no alerts." She looked over at them. "Looks good, we're in."

20

ONLY ONE WINNER

Around one hundred kilometers out from the vast cylindrical city-state of New World One, Luca jacked back into the data-stream and accessed the local navigation beacon network. She was cautious, hanging back, careful to access just the digital terrain around New World One rather than jumping in head-first. It took her only a moment to find the rhythm of the data, find its natural harmony and adjust her own neural frequency to become one with the stream. For a moment she simply let it drift around her and through her, immersing herself in the information flow, finding its resonance. Only then did she dare to begin manipulating it, hoping that the subtlety of her actions would be enough to mask her presence.

She sought out the data set for the ship that had been entered into the traffic control during the handshake. She then deftly reassigned a new set of parameters, making it out to be a maintenance crew ship with its destination being the antennae cluster that Cyrus had identified. To the habitat's systems it was now just a crew embarking on a planned maintenance job to replace one of the microwave dishes. She was tempted to dive further into the data-stream, but caution prevailed. Best not push her luck just yet. There would be time enough for that. She jacked out.

"Okay, we're good. I've set the ship's vector to bring us in close to the antennae cluster."

They watched on the main monitor as the ship closed the gap. Even though they were still some way off, the vast cylindrical habitat soon blocked out the entire view. A proximity alert flashed up on one of the flight systems.

Scott glanced at the readouts. "Looks like a security drone approaching. Checking us out, presumably."

"That's new. Never heard of those being used before," said Cyrus.

"An indication of VanHeilding's paranoia level, I imagine," said Miranda. "Can we see it?"

"On screen now," Luca replied.

A small black dot, silhouetted against the bright skin of the habitat, began to grow in size as it approached. It halted some two hundred meters away and held its position, scanning the ship—no doubt interrogating the preprogrammed flight path of the Xiang Zu vessel. It tracked the ship long enough for Luca to be tempted to jack back into the local grid and find out what it was up to. But it rotated 180 degrees and zoomed off, having satisfied itself that all was as it should be.

Soon, the ship began to adjust its vector to match the spin of the habitat, then started to reduce its forward momentum as it came within sight of the antennae cluster. Reaction thrusters kicked in as it maneuvered into a position approximately one hundred meters from the outer edge of the cluster.

"The access hatch is at the base of that main dish there." Cyrus pointed at the largest of three huge dish array. From a distance, they had seemed small and insignificant. But up close they dwarfed the ship.

"Okay, time to get this party started," Miranda said, as she floated out of the bridge.

A few minutes later, Luca, Miranda, Scott, Cyrus, Rickmann, and two of the Martian crew that had survived the onslaught at the spaceport were suited up and traversing the open space between the ship and the antennae array. Three large storage crates trailed behind on tethers. Luca, like all the others, kept a wary eye out for more security drones as they moved. She touched the suit's gas thruster controls, aiming for the labyrinth of steel beams that supported the motors for the large dish antenna. Ahead of her she could see Miranda and Scott already grappling for a handhold on the superstructure.

One by one they worked their way along the lattice of steel struts until they finally came to the entrance for the maintenance hatch, a wide, tunnel-like gouge set into the skin of the habitat. This was much bigger than Luca had imagined, at least five meters across with a set of double doors at the hatch end. It was a good choice, more than big enough to get the crates into. Once inside that tunnel opening they could power down their suits' thrusters and let the centripetal force of the vast cylinder take over.

They slowly assembled around the hatch entrance and waited for Luca to catch up. She hauled herself forward using a few well-timed bursts of her suit thruster to aid her movement, and finally grabbed a support beam. She moved into the covered tunnel, powered down, and found herself being vacuumed-packed to the roof of the structure. It took her body a few moments to figure out what had happened to it, having spent so long in zero-gee that she was feeling the strain. She hauled herself upright and found that she was standing on the inner roof of the tunnel.

Cyrus signaled to her to come to his location beside the hatch control panel. He had already disassembled the outer cover and showed her a comms port which she could use to jack-in to. Once connected she would then be able to use her neural-lace to directly access the door-locking mechanism and release it without having to expose herself to the wider habitat data-stream. It took her only a few seconds before the hatch doors split open, and they started to shuffle into the airlock, pulling the crates in behind them.

The inner doors scissored open into a wide maintenance tunnel. They were now effectively inside the habitat, with full atmospheric pressure. They all took a few minutes to get accustomed to the new environment before they got out of the bulky EVA suits, which were heavy and clumsy in the artificial gravity they were now experiencing.

"Jeez, that was tougher than I'd thought. I'm so out of

shape." Cyrus stood with one hand resting against the side wall, trying to adjust to the forces now acting on his body.

"Yeah, gravity's a bitch," said Miranda as she finished extracting herself from the suit.

"Luca, time to get this show on the road." Scott scanned the route ahead as he spoke. "Can you check what security sensors are operating down here and disable them?"

"Already done," she replied. "We're good as far as the surface exit point. After that it'll get trickier."

They moved off down along the tunnel, Scott and Cyrus carrying the crate containing the QI core between them. The two Martian crew carried the second crate with the superluminal comms unit. The tunnel was high enough to walk fully upright, with room to spare, and wide enough to walk four abreast. It occupied a space between the outer skin of the habitat and the inner surface. The entire structure was crisscrossed with these tunnels, allowing maintenance crews access to the utility infrastructure that kept the vast space city functioning. They could, in theory, get all the way to the datacenter using only these tunnels, but not all were as commodious as this one. This was a main artery; the off-shoots were much narrower and they would not be able to get the bulky crates through. Therefore, they had no option but to exit out onto the inner surface of the habitat and run the gauntlet.

The tunnel finally opened out into a wide, circular intersection, a point at which several tunnels interconnected. In the center, a broad column rose with a metal staircase on one side and a maintenance lift on the other.

"This is where we exit." Cyrus lowered the crate onto the ground and pointed up toward the top of the column.

It was now game time for Luca, the moment she could no longer put off, the moment when she would see if she really could take on the army of node runners that Fredrick VanHeilding had installed in New World One. She would be exposing herself now, letting them know that she was here, somewhere. They would then scramble to marshal all their combined power to find her and eliminate her. She was now entering a fight to the death, and there would only be one winner.

21

MOBILIZE EVERYTHING

Fredrick VanHeilding fumed as he listened to the report from Cortez Ramirez, commander of the ship he had sent to assist the Xiang Zu Corporation in reacquiring the QI core that they had so incompetently lost. As it turned out, the mercenaries who were currently in possession of the core did not head for the enclave at Elektra. Instead, they were tracked to an old abandoned spaceport in the Berbericia sector, through an intercepted communication from an unknown and unregistered Martian ship.

At the mention of all this, Fredrick could feel pieces of the puzzle he had been grappling with fall into place. So it came as no surprise to him to learn that Miranda and her gang of troublemakers had been on this ship, along with a cohort of Martian military. It was clear from these actions that Mars had sanctioned this mission to repatriate the QI core. How they knew who had it and where to find them was still a mystery to him. Nevertheless, they had all rendezvoused at the abandoned spaceport.

The Xiang Zu fleet were alerted, and three of their ships laid siege to the spaceport with the intention of destroying the entire facility and all on board. But contrary to the deal Fredrick had agreed to with Lui Wei—that being to destroy the QI core—Xiang Zu pushed their luck, halted their bombardment, and instead tried to capture the spaceport intact utilizing a small army of battle-droids.

The VanHeilding ship then lost all contact with the Xiang Zu fleet for over two days before they finally decided to investigate, and what they discovered shook Fredrick to the very center of his being.

Out of nowhere, Luca had shown up in Sebastian's ship, disabled the Xiang Zu fleet, taken control of the battle-droids, and ended the siege in a matter of minutes. Worse, they had all escaped, and taken one of the Xiang Zu ships along with all of the functioning battle-droids. Initial analysis indicated that they were heading for Elektra, as rumors were now spreading within the enclave of a super-weapon coming to help the resistance win the war against the Xiang Zu Corporation.

Fredrick had barely enough time to digest the contents of this report, let alone consider its implications, when an incoming comms alert flashed for Lui Wei. No doubt he had just received the same information at the same time. Fredrick gestured to receive the comms, and a 3D projection of the Xiang Zu official bloomed into life.

"It seems you have not been fully transparent with us, Fredrick." Lui Wei's projection jerked an accusatory finger in his direction.

Fredrick fumed even more at this display of outright arrogance. He pointed an equally accusatory finger at Lui Wei, and spoke through gritted teeth. "I agreed that node-runner resources would be utilized to locate the missing QI core—which you so incompetently lost—on condition that once found, it would be destroyed. It seems to me, Lui Wei, that your people had that chance and failed."

"Failed because you did not inform us of the extraordinary neural capabilities of your estranged granddaughter. Something you chose to hide from us because you are afraid of the chaos she could bring down upon all our heads."

Fredrick was silent for a beat, somewhat taken aback by this accusation.

"However," Lui Wei continued, "as a courtesy to you, I've just received an additional debrief from the commander of the fleet that was engaged in the battle at the Berbericia spaceport. This is something that you are not privy to but nevertheless may be of concern. It would appear that Luca VanHeilding is not on board the ship she stole from your dear departed cousin, but has taken one of ours, and we suspect she is heading for New World One."

Fredrick jerked forward in his seat. "Are you sure?" His voice betrayed his deep concern at this news.

"We correlated a number of visual observations by our crew, and they indicate that she was seen boarding along with the remnants of the Martian crew. The smugglers took Sebastian's ship, along with a number of battle-droids, and they departed in a different direction, we suspect to Elektra. However, the Xiang Zu ship's vector would be consistent with a New World One intercept."

"How long ago?" Fredrick asked, his voice controlled.

"Six Earth-days."

"That means they could be here already," Fredrick mused, his voice betraying a hint of concern.

"Indeed. But just so you know, soon we will commence an all-out assault on the Elektra enclave. We will bring it to heel and all resistance will be crushed. Hopefully you will be able to deal with your problematic family and we can complete the full takeover of the Belt."

Fredrick nodded, and much as he hated to do it, he signed off by thanking Lui Wei for alerting him to Luca's potential arrival at the habitat.

There was no time to waste; he needed to get security ramped up to the highest level—right now. But before he even had time to think, a new comms alert flashed before him, this time from his master node runner.

He gestured to connect. "What is it?"

"She's here," came the reply, simple and to the point.

"Shit, where? Don't tell me she's actually in the habitat?"

"We sensed her in the data-stream a few minutes ago, manipulating the habitat-wide transport system. It's not clear yet where exactly she is or what she's doing."

"Goddamnit, find her!" Fredrick jumped out of his seat and

gesticulated wildly at the projection of the master node runner. "And find that ship."

"What ship would that be, sir?"

Fredrick tried to calm himself down. It would do him no good to be worked up to a point where a rash decision could cost him dearly. He took a deep breath and exhaled, then spoke calmly. "I've been informed that she stole a Xiang Zu ship out at a spaceport in the Berbericia sector. That's how she got here. She threw us a curveball, switching ships and sending Sebastian's to Elektra. Find that ship. It must be here somewhere. Also, she wasn't traveling alone. I think Miranda and her rogue's gallery of associates are also with her, along with several Martian military. You need to find them and find them fast."

The master node runner paused for a moment as he appeared to focus on some inner comms dialogue. "In progress, sir. If they are here, we will find them."

"You had better. Spare no one, and I mean no one. I don't care how hot you run those node runners."

"Yes, sir."

"And I want everything we have mobilized—all military personnel, battle-droids, security drones, everything. Meet me in the operations center in three minutes. And one more thing..."

"Yes, sir. What's that?"

"Make sure the escape ship we discussed is ready to depart, instantly."

"Of course, sir. But I'm sure it won't come to that."

"Really? Then you clearly have no clue as to the threat we are now facing."

He signed off, then smashed his fists down hard onto the holo-table, cracking and splintering the screen. "You have pushed your luck too far, Luca. I will find you and I will destroy you once and for all."

22

THE PERFECT PLACE

L uca sat on the floor and composed herself while the others waited patiently in the maintenance tunnel inter-connector. She focused her mind, jacked-in to the habitat's data-stream, and began to seek out the primary transport AI. With an internal surface area of over six hundred square kilometers, New World One required a complex autonomous transport system to move people and goods around its vast interior. Any disruption to the smooth running of this system could potentially cause chaos—exactly what Luca intended.

It didn't take much to send the transport system into a state of utter confusion. Some careful neurosurgery to the AI's primary algorithm was all it took. Pods no longer stopped where requested; instead they became completely random. That is, all except for one—the pod that would take the crew to the closest drop-off point for the datacenter.

Luca jacked out of the data-stream, stood up, and signaled to the others. "The pod's here." She pointed up toward the overhead exit. "Time to go."

They clambered out of the tunnel inter-connector into a large warehouse used to store a myriad of materials and spare parts for the habitat's subterranean infrastructure. Luca had already deactivated the local security systems so they could move openly and with speed to the main entrance door. This brought them out into a wide-open yard and gave them their first real view of the vast habitat interior.

"It never fails to impress," Cyrus said as he looked up at the opposite side of the cylinder, several kilometers away.

"No time to get all nostalgic, Cyrus." Scott moved over to the waiting transport pod. "This looks like our ride."

It had a flat-bed at the rear, used for transporting goods, and an enclosed passenger cabin at the front. They hauled the crates on first, then clambered into the cabin.

Scott stretched a hand out, gesturing to Luca to get a move on. But instead she took a step back. "Come on, what are you waiting for?" He gestured again.

"Sorry, I'm not coming with you."

"What?" Miranda jumped up from where she was sitting. "No, Luca, what are you doing? We have to stick together."

"I need to create a distraction for you. I need to keep them focused on me. That way you'll have a better chance."

Miranda was about to step back out of the cabin, but the doors closed automatically before she got the chance. Luca looked on as the pod picked up speed and disappeared into a tunnel entrance.

.   .   .

Luca retreated back into the warehouse, sat down on a crate, and focused on the data-stream. It was now time to put her own plan into action and find the exact location of Fredrick VanHeilding. After all, this was the reason she was back here on New World One. It was the mission she had devoted herself to ever since leaving Mars. There would be no more deviations, no more side trips, no more hesitating. She was coming for him now and nothing was going to stop her.

It didn't take her long to sense node-runner activity. They were trying to get a handle on the transport confusion. It was pretty low-grade stuff, yet she wasn't sure if they had any idea of her existence in the network. She delved deeper into the sea of data, searching for her target. His location would be concealed, that much she was sure of. But such was his paranoia that they would create a ring of security around him, in ever-increasing concentric circles. Therefore, Luca searched for this pattern in the data—there couldn't be too many, and one was bound to be protecting him.

As she searched, she noticed a sudden and unexpected burst in node-runner activity. This was accompanied by a pattern shift in the security protocols. Something was happening, something new had occurred. Had the crew been discovered? Yet when she checked, she could see the pod was still on course to arrive at the datacenter in less than a minute.

She went deeper, risking detection, and followed the patterns. It became clear to her that habitat security was being ramped up. Was this as a consequence of the transport chaos?

Possibly, she thought. Yet it seemed like something more, as if new information had come to light. Information that required raising the threat level, and as far as Luca could see, the only thing that could do that was if VanHeilding discovered that her arrival at New World One was imminent or that she was already here. This was not outside the bounds of possibility, yet it did not mean he knew where she was.

Luca needed to move faster, before they started hunting for her in earnest. She began taking more risks, probing deeper into the data-stream, searching for her target. When she eventually found him, he was on the move, heading to the operations center in the administrative sector where primary habitat control was located. He traveled with a cohort of well-trained guards and several security drones.

She estimated it would take her less than thirty minutes to intercept him in the operations center. *The perfect place,* she thought. Where better to trap him and let him watch as his world came tumbling down around him? But before she jacked out and went after him, Luca check on the progress of the crew and realized to her horror that they were about to head into a world of pain.

23

QUANTUM BAY

The pod burst out of the tunnel and into the open as Miranda tried for the fifth time to contact Luca on her comms with no joy. "I just don't understand why she never responds," she said, shaking her head in frustration.

"That's just her way, Miranda," Scott said as he scanned the area. "You should be used to it by now."

The pod came to a halt between stations in the heart of an industrial sector. They were surrounded on all sides by gray, anonymous-looking three-story buildings. Cyrus checked a map display on his visor and pointed to a narrow gap between two buildings. "If we take that route there, we come out at a side entrance to the datacenter. It's the closest entrance to the QI room, the quantum bay."

"Okay, let's get going," said Scott as they piled out of the pod. They hauled the crates out from the back and made their way through the gap between the buildings. They were around halfway along when Luca burst through on general comms.

"Wait up!"

"What?" came Miranda's reply.

The others were halted in their tracks, lowering the crates to the ground and scanning both ends of the narrow route, weapons held high and at the ready.

"I think we've been rumbled," said Luca. "I've detected increased security activity and they've posted additional forces around sensitive sectors, including the datacenter."

"How much more?" asked Scott.

"A lot, including drones and a few droids."

"Jeez, why can't we ever get a break," said Cyrus.

"Hang back for a bit, I'm going to create a distraction. Hopefully it should be enough for you to fight your way in."

"Crap, I knew this wasn't going to be as easy as it sounded." Rickmann nervously scanned their surroundings.

"Okay," said Miranda. "What do you want us to do?"

"Can you see the entrance yet?" Luca asked.

"Not yet. I'll move up a take a look." Miranda nodded to Scott, and the two of them moved up through the gap in the buildings, keeping low until they found some cover behind a low barrier. Miranda took a peek.

The entrance was directly ahead, around one hundred meters. At least eight guards were posted there, that she could see, along with two security drones hovering overhead and two inactive battle-droids.

"That's a crapload of firepower," said Scott as he ducked back behind the barrier.

"I'm going to create some mayhem," said Luca. "You get ready to move when you see an opportunity."

"Okay, got it." Miranda signaled for the others to move up closer, but still keep out of sight.

Over at the entrance to the datacenter, one of the inactive droids began to flicker to life and slowly rise up from its squatting position. The guards all turned to look at it, a little confused as to what it was doing. When it reached full height, its weapons system went live and two shoulder-mounted plasma cannon unfolded from their compartments, took aim at the security drones flying overhead, and fired. The machines crackled and fizzed as their electronics were fried. They plummeted to the ground, smashing into a multitude of pieces.

The droid then turned on the guards, who scattered in multiple directions, some diving for cover, others simply running away as fast as possible. The droid took aim and fired several blasts—none of which hit anyone, but were close enough to get the message across to a few of the braver guards who might be thinking of doing something stupid.

"Okay!" shouted Miranda. "Let's move!"

The area in front of the entrance was now clear of human guards, so they moved as fast as they could with the heavy crates over to main entrance doors, which clicked open for them as they arrived. They bundled themselves into a goods area packed with equipment. The doors shut automatically behind them.

Luca's voice echoed across the general comms channel. "I've activated the second battle-droid and sent both of them on a rampage, heading away from the datacenter. That should keep the guards busy and drag them away from the building. Internal security feeds are also disabled."

"Okay, good work," replied Miranda.

"Just so you know," Luca went on, "I've detected a noticeable ramp up in node-runner activity. They suspect I'm here but they're not sure where, nor what I'm planning. But so far, there's been no indication that they are aware of the QI's existence on the habitat. So I'll keep them focused exclusively on me for as long as I can. Hopefully that should give you enough time to complete the mission."

"So what are you planning, Luca?" Miranda asked. "Are you going after Fredrick?"

"That's always been my plan—you know that. But it's now dependent on that quantum intelligence going online and syncing with the wider QI hive-mind. However, I suspect that even my part in all this is just one element in an even greater plan. One that's been in the making for a very long time."

"Miranda, come on, let's get moving." Scott frantically gestured to her from where he and the others were loading the crates onto a motorized trolley.

"Gotta go, Luca. We won't let you down. Stay safe." Miranda signed off and rushed to catch up with the rest of them.

Cyrus stopped for a second, raising a hand for the others to do likewise. They had passed into a long, narrow corridor with glass walls on either side, behind which were row upon row of server racks all humming with the background noise of coolant fans. He held a hand to his temple, adjusting something on his visor, checking the internal schematic he was using. He pointed down along the corridor. "We need to keep going straight, through two more sets of doors. That will lead us directly to the quantum bay."

They picked up the pace, moving with haste down the long corridor. They almost made it to the end when the door behind them suddenly burst open and several guards came rushing through.

Ferro, one of the Martian crew, was hit by the first blast before anyone even knew what was happening.

"Everybody down!" Miranda shouted as she dropped to the floor and returned fire, followed by Scott and Captain Rickmann. Hudson, the other Martian crew member, began dragging Ferro back behind their hastily formed line.

"Come on, this way, door's open!" Cyrus shouted from the far end of the corridor.

The guards retreated under the onslaught of frantic plasma fire being directed at them. Cyrus hauled the crates out through the door as the others fought a rearguard action. One by one, they backed out the door. Hudson dragged Ferro out first, last was Miranda. Scott and Rickmann pushed at a tall, heavy vending machine, toppling it over and heaving it up against the door, which now crackled and sparked from a barrage of plasma fire.

"Jeez, that was intense." Cyrus wiped a bead of sweat from his brow. "Where the heck did they come from?"

"It was only a matter if time," said Hudson as he helped the injured Ferro to her feet. She was clutching her right thigh. "Can you walk?" he asked.

"Well, I'm sure as hell not hanging around here." She stood up, hopping on one leg.

"We need to keep moving. It isn't going to take them long to get through that door." Miranda glanced back at Scott and Rickmann, who were shoving another vending machine across the door.

They were in a wide, circular atrium that served as a recreation space for the techs working at the facility. In the center was a sunken floor with seating and copious tropical plants. A door suddenly opened to their right, and a startled-looking tech froze when he saw several plasma weapons swing around to face him.

"Beat it!" Scott shouted at him, waving his weapon to emphasize the point.

The tech ducked back inside immediately.

"This way, come on." Cyrus began dragging one of the crates. "I hope this core still functions after all the hammering it's been taking."

They crossed the space and in through another door on the opposite side, leading them into yet another long corridor with rows of server racks on either side. They moved as fast as they could, given Ferro's injury. Miranda took up the rear, expecting at any moment for the door to open and guards to come pouring in. She tried raising Luca on comms but, as usual, she was not responding. They barreled through the final door at the far end and into a wide, circular space. It was sparse and clinical, with a raised dais at its center.

"This is it," Cyrus announced. "Let's get the QI core unpacked."

Ferro sat down on the floor, groaning as she did.

"How long is it going to take, Cyrus?" Miranda asked as she glanced back at the door, aiming her weapon at it.

"As long as it takes, Miranda. I'm an engineer, not a magician."

Miranda sighed. "We can only hold them off for so long."

"I know, I know, now stop talking and let me get on with it."

Luca burst through on general comms. "They've finally figured out what's going on and are trying to cut the power. I'm holding them off for the moment. I'm also keeping the guards busy, but just to warn you, there's a large group heading your way. I'll see what I can do, but be prepared." She signed off again before anyone had a chance to respond.

Scott placed a hand on Cyrus's shoulder. "Okay, buddy. Let's get to work."

They set up a hasty defensive position back outside in the long corridor, utilizing the now empty crates and a few overturned server racks. Scott, Miranda, Rickmann, Hudson, and even the injured Ferro all crouched behind it and waited for the door at the far end to open and all hell to pile through.

Scott and Miranda exchanged a glance. "Here we go again," Scott said with a wink.

24

COMMAND OF ASSETS

Luca worked her way along a series of maintenance tunnels toward the administrative sector, but it was still at least two kilometers away and her progress was being slowed by the narrowness of some of the tunnels, and her need to keep focusing on the data-stream. It was hard to do both at the same time. Every now and again she would have to stop so she could monitor the progress of the others. Each time she did, she could feel more and more node runners being brought to bear on tracking her down. So far she had evaded them, but now they had finally joined up the dots and had a pretty clear idea of what was happening. The QI core was here and would soon be back online.

All sectors were being put into lockdown, all security forces were being mobilized, and all node runners were searching for her. However, the chaos brought about by hacking the transport system was hampering the deployment of security forces, along with several rampaging battle-droids. Yet a strong contingent was closing in on the datacenter even though Luca had several security drones taking pot shots at them. On top of that, several node runners were trying desperately to cut the power to the facility. She needed to stop and deal with the unfolding situation even though security was growing ever tighter around the administrative sector, and every minute she wasted would only make it harder for her to isolate VanHeilding. But she had no choice; she needed that QI core to go online.

She felt the tendrils of a node runner honing in on her as she probed the power system for the datacenter. He must have been a novice because he came straight at her with a neural attack, which Luca swatted away as if it were nothing. Yet now that they had a trace on her, more piled in and it became increasingly problematic for her to ignore it. They left her no option; she pivoted in her mind and bore down on them with as much force as she dared. She swamped their minds with an explosion of neural data, overwhelming the celestial cortex. They backed off, for now, but she knew they would return. This might have been just a test. The next time would be a fight to the death.

But now was not the time for such thoughts, and Luca returned to the task at hand. She isolated the power system from further node-runner intervention by setting up blocks and traps. It should keep them out for a while. Luca then moved on and redirected several battle-droids and security drones to focus their harassment of the security forces in and around the datacenter. Last, she warned Miranda that trouble was coming and that they needed to hurry.

. . .

Luca disengaged from the data-stream and continued on her way. She had progressed another kilometer when the first security drone came hovering down the tunnel. It was so quiet that she hadn't noticed. Fortunately, Fly alerted her in time. It took her a moment to get control of the drone—much too long. It would have had ample time to transmit an alert in the first few seconds of spotting her.

"Crap. They know where we are now, Fly. We need to get out of here quick."

"There is an exit a few meters ahead. Shall I go up and take a look?"

"No wait, I'll use this security drone. If there are any guards on the other side, I'd rather they shoot at it."

"That is greatly appreciated, Luca."

She reached the exit, an overhead hatch accessed by a small set of steps. The drone hovered below. A moment later, she had deactivated the locking mechanism and it began to hinge open. The drone buzzed out.

In her mind's eye she could now see the area around the hatch through the drone's sensors. "All clear," she said after a while. "Let's get out of here."

Luca exited the maintenance tunnel network into a narrow street. She was getting close to the administrative sector, one of the oldest parts of New World One, so this area had a dense, urban feel to it. Although the maximum height of any structure inside the vast habitat was only three stories, the buildings on either side of the street seemed to tower over her. Ahead she could see an intersection, busy with people going about their daily business. But as she turned out onto the main street, she got a sense that they were all frustrated by the transport chaos and the subsequent sector lockdown imposed by the habitat security. Fly rose high into the air and Luca could now get a better sense of how far she still had to go.

The administrative buildings had a cordon of security around them—guards, droids, multiple airborne drones. Another contingent was moving down along the street toward her location, presumably coming to investigate the exit, now that she had been sighted close by.

She dodged behind a group of pedestrians, following for a bit until she had the opportunity to cross the street without being spotted. Overhead, Fly tagged several security drones also heading her way. She stepped into the cover of a doorway and entered the data-stream again. This time she could feel a heightened intensity in the data, as if the entire habitat was experiencing a rush of digital adrenaline—it fizzed with frenetic activity. She took control of the security drones that Fly had tagged and rerouted them toward one of the entrances to the administrative sector.

They swooped down low and buzzed the security guards, who dived out of the way. Luca checked the drone's weapons systems. Pulsed Energy Projectile set to nonlethal for crowd control, fully charged and good for approximately twenty rounds each. She dialed up the intensity, which should be enough to incapacitate an average adult for an hour or so, maybe longer. But this gave her only five rounds per drone. *Should be enough,* she thought.

The guards had resumed their positions, this time keeping an eye on the hovering drones. Luca fired. Five incandescent balls of plasma energy shot out of the drones, hitting all five guards. All dropped like stones. She ran for the entrance, and Fly followed along with several of the security drones, all now under her control.

Luca entered into a high glass atrium. Two startled guards jumped up from a control desk, until they too were blasted by a drone. On her left was the elevator that would take her up to the top floor; from there she planned to get out onto the flat roof of the building. She should be able to get all the way to the operations center, where Fredrick VanHeilding huddled with his security team. She sent the drones back outside the building to give her cover when she exited up top.

As the elevator rose, she took a moment to jack-in and check on the situation at the datacenter. A grueling firefight was taking place in the corridor outside the quantum bay. Scott looked injured; he was holding his weapon with just one hand. Several guards were also down. "Shit," Luca said out loud.

"What's the matter?" said Fly, who had taken up a position on the roof of the elevator, clinging to a vent.

"The others need help, and fast. Too much going on all at once." Luca searched the local area for assets she could utilize to bring to bear on the fight going on outside the quantum bay, but as soon as she began probing the data-stream, several node runners materialized and began to coordinate a data block. This was a new strategy. Rather than take her on directly, they were combining their neural power in an effort to counter her control of the data-stream, and it was working. Luca found herself getting bogged down, wasting time that she didn't have. She pulled out just as the elevator reached the top floor and the doors opened, having failed to take command of any assets.

Fly went ahead to scout out the route that would bring Luca out onto the roof. When it reported back *all clear,* Luca made her way to the ladder and exited out onto the roof. Overhead she could see the security drones she had commandeered earlier waiting for her. Luca now gave them new instructions: to fly to the datacenter, gain access to the quantum bay, and attack the security guards laying siege to it. She watched as they moved off at maximum speed, hoping they would get there in time.

Luca turned back to scan the roof area only to see two battle-droids clambering across the flat terrain toward her at speed. She considered recalling the security droids, but realized it was too late for that as the first plasma blasts smashed down around her.

She dove for the roof hatch, tumbling back down through the opening, and landing hard on the floor below with a grunt. She picked herself up and ran for cover through an open door. Fly was still aloft, so she could see in her mind's eye the two droids making for the roof hatch. Behind them, two more droids climbed onto the roof, followed by a third.

"Luca, more battle-droids coming your way. I count five altogether," said the micro-drone.

"I see them, Fly, I see them."

"Regrettably, my weapons system is ineffective against such adversaries."

Luca took a moment to compose herself, breathing slowly. There was no way out of this by running; she would have to get control of one or more of those droids, and that meant facing off against a more formidable node-runner army. She stood her ground and focused on the data-stream.

The assault was instantaneous, a barrage of focused neural data rushing into her cerebral cortex. A sensory overload so intense that she had difficult simply standing upright. She let out a groan, clasped her head with both hands, and slowly slumped to the floor—such was the ferocity of the neural attack. And worse, somewhere in the depths of all the signal noise she sensed one of the droids had dropped through the roof hatch. It was now in the corridor, only moments away from finding her.

Luca needed to get a grip on the attack, and fast. She took a deep breath and stopped fighting the neural assault. Instead she fought down her panic and let the data-stream wash over her, seeking out its frequency. She soon found its resonance and began to ride the wave. Where before she was drowning in a sea of neural chaos, she found that she could now shift and bend with it, working her way toward an understanding of its waveform, and slowly she began to generate her own opposing frequency. This she grew in intensity, building its amplitude until at last it started to cancel out the attack. The droid appeared in the open doorway, scanning the room for her location.

The node-runner attack began to falter. The intensity was

too much for some of the weaker minds that had been seconded into the assault. Luca could feel them becoming overwhelmed and the harmonics of their minds turning one by one into white noise—brain death.

A second droid had now reached the doorway as the first began to move into the room, scanning for her life-form as it entered.

The tsunami in her head began to build as Luca countered the attack, folding it back against itself and directing it outward onto the node-runner hive mind. Luca tweaked its resonance, creating a feedback loop that grew and multiplied exponentially until she finally felt it crash against their collective neural consciousness.

All was quiet, save for a low background hiss of neural static.

Luca then broke through into the data-stream proper, seeking out control of the battle-droid that was only meters away from her. But it had already found her, zeroing in on her location and priming its plasma weapon.

"Run, Luca. I cannot hold it off much longer," Fly's voice burst into her mind. The little drone frantically hovered in front of the droid's targeting system, preventing it from acquiring a lock on Luca. The droid tried to reposition itself, but each time the drone would shift and buzz. In frustration, it fired on the drone.

"No." Luca screamed. "Fly!"

But the drone didn't answer.

The droid retargeted its weapon system, this time on Luca.

But it was too late; she had finally acquired control. It disengaged and instead turned a full 180 degrees and unleashed a barrage of fire on the second droid entering through the open doorway.

Luca stood up, a little unsteadily, using a hand against the wall to balance herself. She heard a buzz and the little drone hovered into view.

"Fly, you're alive."

"Not in the strict sense of the word, but I am still functioning, if that is what you mean."

"I thought the droid vaporized you."

"That machine has a ponderously slow mind in comparison to the hyper-agility of my neural network. I almost feel sorry for it."

Luca took a few slow breaths to calm herself down and refocus on external events. The QI was still not fully online, and the fight had reached a point of desperation, as they had now abandoned the hallway and retreated inside the quantum bay. But there was still hope. The assault had been slowed by the pileup of bodies in the narrow corridor and the security drones had just entered the building, felling anyone and anything that got in their way.

There was also a noticeable absence of node-runner activity. Had she eliminated them all? The thought frightened her. Were they all now brain dead? But there was no time to reflect on this; Fredrick VanHeilding was still her target, and if he sensed the tide was turning then he may try and escape. She needed to hurry.

"Time to go," she said to the drone. "Back out onto the roof. This time I think we'll bring a few of our own battle-droids, even if they are slow and ponderous."

25

THE SIGNAL

Dakota ran a hand over the sleek surface of the command console on the bridge of Daedalus. He had never been in a ship so luxurious, so well crafted, so expensive. He found it hard to believe that such ships existed and wondered at the kind of wealth that was needed to commission such a craft. It was obscene in his mind. Yet, it was his now, so he better get used to it.

He strapped himself into the commander's chair, upholstered in real leather hide, a material so expensive that he had only ever seen an example in a museum. The rest of the crew were also having difficulty coming to terms with the gross extravagance of the ship. They were floating on the bridge, looking, touching, and generally shaking their heads in disbelief.

"Well screw me sideways with a big stick, would you look at that." Aeon had activated the forward monitor that blossomed to life with a 230-degree perspective of space, directly forward of the ship. The clarity was astounding; it felt like they could float out into the vastness.

"We should have kept the QI core, Cap," Angus said as he strapped himself into another of the command seats. "I still don't see why we let the Martians have it."

"It's better with them—they know how to get it online, they know what they're doing." Dakota gestured at the console embedded in the seat's armrest.

"They'll never get it into New World One," Angus continued. "Not even with that weird psycho-girl they have."

"That weird psycho-girl, as you call her, saved all our asses. If not for her, we'd all be floating out in the void. If anyone can get them inside New World One, it'll be her."

"We should have persuaded her to join the fight on Elektra, that's where this is all going down," said Aeon. "Screw New World One, they're just a bunch of pussies. They never even tried to put up a fight."

Dakota ignored her and instead scanned the camera feeds. The final loading had been complete, everybody was on board including the dead and injured crew from the battle. Those that hadn't made it out with their lives were stored in one of the cargo holds; their families would be informed once they got to Elektra—if they got to Elektra. The injured were being treated in the state-of-the-art medbay on board. Most, if not all, would be back and ready for action in no time.

They had also acquired a dozen or so of the Xiang Zu battle-droids, which the Martian tech had assured him could be controlled from the bridge of Daedalus. Brooker was already working on this, testing out the interface. They would be a very useful asset to have in the forthcoming battle.

"If everybody is finished moaning and complaining, can we get this show on the road?" Dakota called out over the general comm.

"All on board, Cap. Everything stowed away, ready for departure," Angus responded.

"Well, okay then. Let's get going." He pointed at the vast expanse of space displayed on the panoramic bridge monitor.

Alerts sounded, warning the crew to get strapped in. The ship began to hum, building in intensity as the engines came up to full power. It moved forward, gently at first, clearing the area of the old spaceport. Then began to accelerate, increasing thrust until almost everybody on board blacked out with the gee forces.

Elektra, classified as a minor planet in the Belt, was unique in that it was the only known quadruple asteroid system. It had three satellites, thought to be shards of the main body, blown out by some major impact in the ancient past. It was approximately two hundred and fifty kilometers at its widest point and, as such, had a feeble gravitational pull compared to Earth, or even Ceres.

So when people referred to the population center of Elektra, they were not referring to the primary asteroid body— they were referring instead to an assembly of space stations that had grown up within the quadruple system. Few people existed on the surface of Elektra, only miners and support staff, and then for only brief periods of time.

This amalgam of space habitat infrastructure had grown over the years into the second largest population center in the Belt. It was a hodgepodge of habitats that now accommodated some twenty thousand fiercely independent people, who were all preparing to fight to maintain that independence.

Daedalus slowed to a parking coordinate behind S/2003, a six-kilometer-diameter satellite of the primary Elektra asteroid, approximately fifteen hundred kilometers away from the main center of population. This, Dakota reckoned, would give them some time to scout out the approach with the least possibility of being spotted.

They had made the journey in half the time it would have taken in his old ship, so chances were good that the Xiang Zu fleet encircling the enclave would still be in the dark as to the outcome of the battle for the old spaceport. Yet, arriving in a stolen VanHeilding ship, particularly one that had belonged to a high-ranking member of the family, would almost certainly prompt interception and investigation.

Dakota, Angus, Aeon, and some of the other crew gathered around the central holo-table on the ship's bridge, studying a real-time asteroid map of the local region. In the center was the space station enclave of Elektra with the primary asteroid looming large behind it. A multitude of illuminated dots illustrated the locations of several ships, all stationary relative to the enclave.

"Which ships are Xiang Zu?" Dakota asked, pointing at the dots.

"All of them," Aeon replied.

"Holy cow, that's a lot of hardware!" Angus exclaimed. "Where did they get so many?"

"Screwing over other families' mining infrastructure all over this region of the Belt and taking their assets, including ships," said Aeon, waving a hand at the dots. "That's why it's such a mixed bag. We're talking freighters, transports, tugs, even a barge or two. They stick a few cannon on them and press them into service."

Dakota nodded. "I think we need to contact the resistance on Elektra directly and find out what's going on, see if they have a plan. We don't want to go in there all guns blazing and end up screwing things up."

"There's no way communications will go unnoticed," Brooker interjected.

"True." Dakota nodded. "But direct comms with my brother might."

The crew looked from one to the other; no one spoke.

"Keep an eye on things. I'll be in the state room—there's good comms there." Dakota pushed himself away from the holo-table and out from the bridge.

Dakota had refused to use Sebastian's staterooms as his quarters on board Daedalus, regarding them as way too ostentatious for his humble tastes. Instead he had taken a less commodious cabin on the lower decks, beside where his crew were located. However, the comms setup Sebastian had implemented in his quarters were the best on the ship, excluding the bridge. And this was a conversation he preferred to keep private, as it had been quite some time since he and his brother had talked. He wasn't even sure if he could still contact him, and even if he did, that his brother would take the call. But he had to try, and now was the time.

He strapped himself into a plush seat in the stateroom, connected his personal area data network to the ship's AI, and instructed it to seek out the contact location of his brother, Quinn.

It didn't take long. Less that minute later he was face-to-face with a hazy holographic projection of Quinn, sitting in a darkened room with what looked to Dakota like a group of fighters, waiting for the shit to go down. His face wore a tired, beaten look. The look of a man twice his age.

"Hello, brother. I see you've been doing well for yourself. Nice digs you've got there," Quinn almost sneered.

Dakota glanced around reflexively at the luxurious interior of the ship's stateroom. "Don't let this fool you, Quinn. It's not mine."

"Stolen, I presume." Quinn raised an eyebrow.

Dakota hesitated for a beat. "Eh...yes, but not by me."

"Figures." His brother sighed. "So what you want this time? If you're looking for a place to hide out again, you can forget it. Go and take your troubles somewhere else. We're sick of taking the heat for your wrecking-ball lifestyle."

"No, believe it or not, this time I'm here to help."

Quinn gave a half-hearted snort. "Really? You...actually help?"

Dakota became silent. His head lowered, and he fingered the edging of the seat. "I'm not the person you think I am, at least, not anymore. There comes a time in a man's life when he gets to thinking about what really matters." Dakota gave a dismissive wave of his hand. "Ah...maybe I'm getting old, I don't know. But it came to me that I needed to pick a side." He looked at his brother. "So I'm here to fight. Fight for what's right."

It was Quinn's turn to go silent. He gave a barely audible sigh and pushed his unkempt hair back off his forehead. "I suppose we're all getting old. But if what you're telling me is true, then all I can say is...I'm very glad to have you on our side. God knows we could do with it. I don't know how much longer we can hold out against this blockade—we're living off fumes here." He gave a strained smile.

"All is not as hopeless as you think, Quinn." He leaned closer to the projection, and spoke in almost hushed tones. "There is a person...a person that possesses a power beyond anything I could ever have imagined. I've seen this firsthand, seen what she can do." He waved a hand around. "It was she who gave me this ship."

Quinn's eyes widened, his voice low. "I've heard some of these stories before. But they're just myths, bar talk for old drunks who want to sound profound. Are you saying these stories are real?"

"Believe it, brother. She's not a myth."

"Well, I'll be damned." Quinn shook his head and ran a hand through his thick hair again. "Will she help us?"

"After a fashion. Her beef is with Fredrick VanHeilding back on New World One, that's where she's heading along with a number of others who have a quantum intelligence core that was, eh...stolen a few months back. Their mission is to get it back online. If they pull that off, then they'll be helping us indirectly. With a QI back in control of this region, Xiang Zu's wings will be clipped."

Quinn's face morphed into a look of astonishment. "Is this true? Can a quantum intelligence do all they say it can, or is it just another myth?"

Dakota shook his head. "That, I honestly don't know. All I can say is, smarter people than you or I believe so. They think getting it back online can end this war. And maybe it will. Then again, maybe it won't, or they'll fail in the attempt. What I'm saying is we still need to take the fight to Xiang Zu, regardless."

Quinn gave his estranged brother a considered look. "What've you got in mind?"

"Who runs the show down there? Who's in command?"

"It's a bit of a hodgepodge of different groups. Nobody has faced this before. But Central are the ones that most people look to to take the lead."

"Can you contact them?"

"Yeah, we're pretty tight, good communications. But you still haven't told me what you're planning."

"I'm planning to do what I always do in these types of situations—shoot first and clean up the mess later." He gave a wink. "Xiang Zu are just sitting and waiting, so we take them now, while they least expect it. This ship is state of the art: very fast, highly maneuverable, and well-armed. We also have a dozen battle-droids under my command. So, the plan is to go in hard and fast. What you need to do is convince Central to send out any ships you have to join the battle. We could take them." Dakota held a clenched fist up in front of him.

"Jeez, I don't know." Quinn screwed his mouth up. "We've got no battleships or anything like that. All we got are barges and tugs with a few plasma cannon strapped onto the hull."

"That's all we need. Xiang Zu's fleet isn't much better. Most of them have been grabbed from the outposts."

"Central will take some convincing to get them to row in with that plan. Their strategy is all about defense."

"But you'll try?"

Quinn gave a reluctant nod. "Yeah, I'll try."

"Good. Tell them to get ready, tell them to wait for my signal."

"What's the signal?"

Dakota gave a wry smile. "Mayhem, brother. Mayhem."

26

SYSTEM GLITCH

F redrick VanHeilding paced around the operations center in New World One at the same time as watching a cascade of chaos unfold across the habitat, and beyond. It had taken some time to unpack the seeming random pattern of transportation lockdowns, rogue security drones, rampaging battle-droids, and datacenter hacks into a clear picture of what the heck was going on. But now it had become real. Luca was here, in the habitat, and she was coming for him. Worse, she had been aided by her treacherous mother, Miranda, and a group of Martian military, who were currently attempting to activate the stolen QI core inside the habitat's primary datacenter.

Battles seemed to rage everywhere, none more fiercely than inside the datacenter itself, where Miranda and her scumbag comrades were holding his security forces at bay with the aid of several compromised battle-droids and security drones. This was something that could not be allowed to happen. If that QI were to become active, then things would get a lot more difficult for VanHeilding, not to mention his partners in this venture, the Xiang Zu Corporation. Therefore, more and more forces were being allocated to the data-center battle.

That was until Luca finally showed up in the data-stream. She had given away her location and by doing so had become top priority. If she could be cornered and killed, then the data-center battle would be over in seconds. Battle-droids, security drones, and armed forces all now rushed to her location to engage.

But Fredrick was under no illusions as to just how formidable an opponent Luca really was. She was an extremely powerful node runner, but there must be a limit to how much she could control and manipulate at any one time. Already she was controlling the transportation lockdown as well as multiple battle-droids and security drones at several different locations all over the vast habitat. If she could be further engaged by a battle group, then that could give his own node runners the opportunity to finally take her on in the data-stream and ultimately take her down, once and for all.

As Fredrick glanced across the operations center area, he could see them all jacking in and getting ready to engage. One-on-one they were no match for her, but as a collective they stood a chance, particularly when Luca's mind was utilizing so much of its bandwidth to manipulate the ongoing chaos.

He waited anxiously, pacing the area, and flashing quick glances at the incoming data on the display monitors. It didn't help that some admin tech had managed to obtain a feed from the battle raging out at the mining enclave of Elektra. To Fredrick's horror, he realized that it was being broadcast from the bridge of Sebastian VanHeilding's ship, Daedalus. The one that Luca had stolen back on Mars. His rage was at a boiling point. This was the ultimate insult to his family name. A VanHeilding ship attacking the Xiang Zu fleet. It showed a mass of junkyard ships all moving out from Elektra to engage the blockaders, all to the soundtrack of a mercenary captain spewing out rebel propaganda on an open broadcast.

"Turn that goddamn feed off!" VanHeilding's voice bellowed across the operations area. A timid admin tech tapped an icon on his console. The feed went dead.

"We have her, sir. She's on the run. Droids are closing in." The main screen in the room flickered to a camera feed from a droid. It was not far from this location and showed several plasma blasts screeching across a rooftop, and Luca disappearing down a hatch. The droid moved fast, reaching the hatch and dropping down after her. Several more droids follow behind.

So far she had not tried to take control of them; she was running scared, she knew what was waiting for her if she tried to jack-in to the data-stream. VanHeilding glanced over at the node runners. "Don't let me down this time," he said to himself.

The droid scanned the corridor, flipped to infrared, and found a heat signature a few rooms away. Luca had finally run out of road; she was trapped between the prospect of a neural onslaught from a collective node-runner assault or the high-energy blast from a droid cannon. He held his breath.

Suddenly there was a power drop in the room, the lights dimmed for a split-second, screens glitched, projections flickered. VanHeilding instinctively glanced over to where the node runners were jacked-in. Something was happening.

"She's in," a tech shouted out. "She's jacked-in."

On the main monitor, the droid drew ever closer to the heat signature. But VanHeilding wasn't interested in seeing it. His concern now was with the node runners. He rushed into the runner bay and looked at the biometrics; all were running hot. *Holy crap,* he thought, *she's actually taking them on—all of them.*

Alerts squealed out from one of the node-runner bays as the biometrics flatlined, then another, and another. VanHeilding backed away as more succumbed to brain death.

He looked back at the main monitor; the droid looked down on the writhing figure of Luca. "Take the shot, take the goddamned shot!" he screamed at the monitor. But the view changed. The droid swung around, flipped back to the visual spectrum, and blasted a second droid that was following close behind.

Fredrick VanHeilding froze, his eyes fixed on the screen. Over in the node-runner bay, biometric alarms screeched. Slowly he began to think the unthinkable—maybe he was going to need that escape ship after all.

"Sir," a tech called over, "the QI core has been activated and is commencing a data-sync."

"Has it gained control yet?" His voice sounded feeble.

"No, sir. It will take time to become fully operable."

"How long?"

"Eh." The tech consulted the data monitors. "Best guess, ten to fifteen minutes."

That might be enough, he thought. But he had no time to lose. Already the battle-droid, now under Luca's control, was moving toward the main entrance of the operations center. It was time to get out, and fast.

27

MOTOR SKILLS

Luca sensed the quantum core go online, sensed it seeking out its brethren across the system at superluminal speeds. And with the data-stream within New World One now free of node-runner activity, she was free to roam where she wanted. *Have I killed them all?* she wondered. Yet, she knew it was not good for her to dwell on this. No good could come of it, best move on and finish the job.

She opened a comms channel with Miranda. "How you all holding up?"

Miranda replied in breathy, staccato sentences. "QI online, but Scott's badly injured, still hanging in there."

"Security forces have backed off from the datacenter," said Luca. "Too many droids and drones defending it now. Looks like the battle is over for you."

"Cyrus says QI still syncing."

"Yeah, I noticed. Another ten minutes or so and it will have full control, game over. I'll get a medical team to your location."

"Where are you?"

"Oh, I'm on a mission. There's a rat I have to track down and take care of, but I don't think it'll be too much of a problem. Gotta go, catch you later." She signed off.

Luca had sent several battle-droids to the operations center, more as a distraction than as an attempt to snare Fredrick VanHeilding. She knew that once he saw the QI go online, he'd figure his time was up and make a run for it. And now that the data-stream was free of node runners, Luca could track him and follow at her leisure.

He was heading for a small, fast ship that was docked to the exterior hull of the New World One habitat, not far from the operations center. It was an escape ship that would be flung clear, due to the habitat's spin, by simply disengaging the docking port. It didn't even need to power up its engines.

Luca could see him via a camera feed jogging down the long corridor. A security drone flew overhead, and behind him followed by a battle-droid and two others of VanHeilding's entourage. But as he passed a set of fire doors, Luca activated them, slamming them shut and isolating VanHeilding in the corridor. He stopped, looked back at the doors, and cursed. He started banging at the control panel, to no avail. He turned back and ran for the ship, alone.

Luca looked at Fly. "Well, the time has come. Are you ready?"

"I am always ready, Luca."

"Okay, then. Let's get this done."

. . .

VanHeilding's escape ship could not detach from the habitat without disengaging the docking mechanism, and Luca had control of that. So no matter what VanHeilding tried, he could not escape. Yet, as Luca approached the ship's access hatch, she needed to be on high alert. A trapped rat could be a formidable foe. She stood to one side of the hatch and gave the command to open it. As she suspected, a barrage of plasma fire burst out. Luca nodded to Fly, and the little drone entered.

She heard more plasma fire and then silence. A moment later, Fly flew out again. "Done. You can come in now."

Luca stepped onto the ship and made her way to the cockpit. There, slumped on the control seat, was Fredrick VanHeilding, his head tilted to one side, a small barb protruding from his neck.

Luca reached over and plucked it out. "Is he still aware?" she asked Fly.

"Yes. I only shot him with a low dose. He can't move, but he's still awake."

Luca moved in front of the paralyzed VanHeilding, adjusted his head so it was upright in the seat, and looked directly into his eyes. She could see the rage in there as he struggled to move. But he was very much aware; his eyes blinked a few times.

"So, my dear grandfather, I believe you wanted to see me? Well, here I am." She sat down in an adjacent seat and looked up at the wraparound monitor that served as the front window of the ship. It currently displayed exactly what would be seen if it was indeed a true window. The vast, gleaming expanse of the habitat's hull bisected the view. Above it was the blackness of space.

"Planning on leaving us, just when things were getting interesting?" She looked over at Fredrick. A pained expression was etched on his face, his breathing labored.

Luca returned to gazing at the view. "You know, you completely screwed my life up." Her voice was low, matter-of-fact. "You turned me into a monster, someone most people fear. As for the others? Well, they think I'm a god, a deity to be worshipped." She looked over at Fredrick again. He blinked.

"How can I live in this world anymore? How can I be... normal?" She held his gaze for a beat. "You did this. You and your family and your genetics corporation. I was just another experiment to you, like so many before me, I imagine." She gave a sigh. "Still, what's done is done, and neither you nor I, nor your screwed-up corporation, can change that, can we?"

The corners of Fredrick's eyes seemed to tighten.

"Nevertheless, you must pay the price. And so there's a little show I've prepared for you."

Luca disengaged momentarily from her one-sided conversation with her grandfather and jacked-in to the data-stream. The QI had finished its sync. It was now fully integrated into the QI hive-mind and communicating across the system at superluminal speeds, enabling Luca to contact Athena back on Earth in real time.

Luca, glad to see you are still alive and well, the soft sonorous voice of the QI resonated in her head.

"Thank you, Athena, so am I. Are we ready to activate the plan?"

Yes, everything is still in place.

"Do we have a satellite over the area?"

I took the liberty of repositioning one with an excellent high-resolution camera feed. It is ready when you are.

"Very well, let the show begin." Luca shifted her mind back to Fredrick VanHeilding. His head had drooped to one side.

"You need to pay attention to this." She leaned over and unceremoniously jerked his head upright and wedged it into the seat's headrest. "That's better. Wouldn't want you to miss seeing this." Luca pointed at the screen.

With that, the view on the panoramic screen changed to an aerial view of the VanHeilding Corporation's subarctic research lab. The image was blurry at first but quickly flicked into focus.

Fredrick gave an audible groan.

"Fly, how soon before that curare wares off?" Luca studied her grandfather's face.

"Full motor function restored in approximately forty-five minutes depending on body mass, etcetera. But it's a gradual process, so expect some feeble movement from around the ten-minute mark."

"Hmmm." Luca screwed her mouth up. Then took out her plasma pistol, set it to stun, and placed it on her lap with the muzzle pointing at Fredrick. She patted his arm. "Just don't try anything stupid. Okay?" Luca waved the pistol at him.

Fredrick didn't answer.

"You know this place, I think." She pointed at the image on the screen. "It's your primary research facility. The place where you keep all the knowledge that makes your corporation and your family one of the most powerful in the system." She glanced over at him to make sure he was paying attention.

"You see, when I killed your moronic cousin Sebastian, and stole his ship, all I wanted to do was come here and kill you. But then I got to thinking. I realized that it wouldn't be true justice, considering what you did to me, how you robbed me of normality, and turned me into a freak to be experimented on. So I thought, what could I take from you that would redress the balance? And the answer was to take away all that gives you and your corrupt family power. So I set in motion a plan to do exactly that." She pointed at the screen again. "Watch."

The satellite feed showed movement around the facility. Something was happening; several technical vehicles were snaking their way to the entrances of main buildings: fire trucks, medical units, people transports. As all this was happening, Luca continued.

"It started with a conversation I had with Xenon Hybrid on Mars." Luca glanced over at VanHeilding, who seemed to be sitting a bit more upright in the seat. "You've heard of him, I'm guessing. He's kind of a weird character, ancient, and possibly not even Homo sapiens. But he told me a very interesting thing: that every single genetic breakthrough and patent that the VanHeilding Corporation possesses was based on technology stolen from Mars. Which, if true, means that you and your corporation don't own shit." She looked back to Fredrick to see if he was getting all this. His eyes had a distinctly angry look. Luca nodded and returned to the screen. "So I broke into this facility a while back and had a good long look through your state secrets, and guess what I found? That's right, everything Xenon had told me was true."

By now the satellite feed was showing masses of workers hurrying out of the facility and piling onto waiting transports.

"So I stole it all, and right this very minute it's being disseminated out across the grid." She looked over at VanHeilding again. "That's right, every science lab in the entire system now has access to all that research. You no longer have the monopoly, now everybody has it."

Fredrick VanHeilding seemed to bare his teeth and struggled to expel a long, angry, guttural sound. On screen, the last of the people had been evacuated from the facility and the transports began moving off up the valley to the accommodation blocks. Tents were being set up, with teams in hazmat suits ready to process the people when they arrived.

"But I did more than just release all your research." Luca pointed at the screen. "They're all evacuating because of a Level Four bio-leak alert. But don't worry, it's a false alarm, it's just to get everyone to leave the area." She again looked over to VanHeilding, who had now regained enough motor skills to contort his face into a look of horror. "Now, I want you to watch very, very carefully. See"—Luca pointed at the screen—"they're all out, and up at the evacuation point. Okay, Athena, do it now."

For a moment, nothing happened. Then the ground directly over the subterranean facility began to crumple inward, creating a hundred-meter-wide dip. Then it exploded outward in a sudden release of violent energy. The blast rippled across the screen. Dust and rubble flew high into the air, obscuring the view. The satellite image pulled back to show a massive cloud of dust covering most of the site.

"And poof! It's all gone." Luca snapped her fingers.

VanHeilding groaned and gurgled and struggled to move his paralyzed body.

Luca granted him a contemptuous look as he withered in his seat. "All gone. Your empire is no more, everything that made your corporation, and your family, what they were is now free for anyone who wants it. And your...oh-so-precious research labs are nothing more than a cloud of dust."

She raised herself off the seat and stood up. "Well, I enjoyed our little chat, but I'm going to leave you now. Things to do, people to meet. And I don't want to delay you from wherever it is you're planning on going in this ship. But just so you know, I've disabled the ship's power." She leaned over him. "And you're kinda stuck in that seat for a while, so good luck figuring out how to survive past the next hour or so."

Luca walked off the ship to the frantic, guttural groans of Fredrick VanHeilding. She shut the outer hatch, and released the ship from its dock. It spun off the hull of the habitat and out into deep space.

28

SUMITOMO SHIPYARD

Scott ran through a few preliminary flight checks as he waited for Cyrus to arrive. *What's keeping him?* he thought. The small shuttle craft was next-gen Martian tech, so his checks weren't really necessary; he was more interested in finding out what this craft was capable of. He glanced out through the cockpit window across the spaceport apron and the great domes of Jezero City on Mars. *It's a good place to live*, he thought to himself. He had been in far worse places. They knew how to look after people here.

An alert flashed on the dash console indicating the outer airlock door had been activated, and a moment later Cyrus entered the cabin. He unclipped his EVA suit helmet and gloves, climbed into the cockpit, and sat down beside Scott.

"You made it," said Scott. "For a moment I thought you weren't coming."

"Sorry, I was looking for a rust bucket. I didn't think they'd let you loose on something this fancy." He rubbed a hand along the exquisitely upholstered arm rest. "Nice."

"Ha, actually I bought it. It's a former Xiang Zu family shuttle. Got it as part of their reparations settlement. It has a stupidly overpowered fusion reactor with enough juice to generate its own radiation shield. Ridiculous for a craft of this size."

"Does it make coffee?"

Scott glanced over at his buddy with a wry smile. "Actually, it does. You just ask it."

"Stop, I'm getting envious." Cyrus settled into the seat and strapped himself in. "So, where's this old boneyard you want to show me?"

"It's not too far, we'll be there in twenty minutes." Scott gestured at the control screen and the craft began to gently lift off from the pad. It rotated around sixty degrees in midair before increasing power to its main engines, and then began to rise up through the Martian atmosphere.

"Say, how you getting on with that new arm?" Cyrus gestured with his left arm.

Scott glanced down at his own left hand and wiggled his artificial fingers. "A bit weird. It feels kinda like a real arm, so much so that sometimes I forget and end up crushing something." He looked over at Cyrus and waved. "Almost better than the real thing." He laughed.

The battle at the datacenter on New World One had been brutal. Wave after wave of security guards had tried to breach their defenses, and each time they'd fought them back. The tide eventually turned in their favor when the security drones and battle-droids that Luca had commandeered entered the building. But this was not before the last wave of attacks had blown open the heavy metal security door to the quantum bay, which slammed down on Scott's left arm just below the elbow, crushing it so badly that the excruciating pain made him pass out. He awoke in a hospital bed, with only one-and-a-half arms and a body covered in bandages.

But the QI core had been activated, the fighting ceased, the VanHeilding family had been vanquished, and the vast habitat city slowly began to be reclaimed by the original governing council. Yet for Scott, it was all a kind of background blur until they had finally arrived back on Mars. The bio-techs at the Xenon Institute went to work and fabricated a prosthesis to replace his lost arm. He had a neural implant fitted which would, theoretically, give him full motor control over his new limb and hand. But it took a while to get it all dialed in.

It was during one of these *tuning* sessions at the institute when Dr. Yastika Parween informed him, in a strangely disconcerting tone, that they could now regrow him a new biological arm. It would be as if he'd never lost it in the first place.

Scott took a moment to digest this bombshell, glancing down a few times at his current robotic limb, and asked the obvious question. "How come you're telling me this now and not back a few months ago, before all this happened?" He raised his prosthesis and waved it at Dr. Parween.

"We simply couldn't do it back then. Yes, we knew it was

theoretically possible, but there were a number of technical roadblocks. Then Luca released all that VanHeilding Corporation bio-tech research into the wild and we finally had the answers. Not just to the process of regenerating human body parts, but a whole treasure trove of new medical science. Extraordinary." She gestured expansively. "It will be like you never lost it, exactly as before, maybe just a slight scarring at the join."

Dr. Parween looked at Scott, expecting an answer. When he didn't reply immediately, the doctor continued. "It's an incredible thing she did. We're entering a new age, a new era of medical science. And to think VanHeilding was sitting on all this, doling it out piecemeal just to maximize control. Hard to believe, really." She shook her head.

Scott wiggled the fingers of his bionic hand. "Let me think about it. I've only just got used to this, so I can't quite wrap my brain around it yet."

"Oh course, of course. There's no rush. Anytime you like. It will always be there for you should you decide to do it."

Scott gestured at the dash console, and a 3D projection blossomed to life on the central holo-screen in the shuttle's cockpit. He pointed at the rotating image. "That's what I want you to check out."

Cyrus glanced at the image for a brief second before looking over at Scott. "The Sumitomo Shipyard? That's where we're going?"

"Yup." He nodded.

"Jeez, you take me to all the best places." He studied the projection for a moment. "That's a Xiang Zu enterprise, isn't it?"

"Not anymore. It's been handed over to the Martian state as part of their reparations settlement. And Mars wants to pass the lease on to someone else."

Cyrus cocked his head at Scott and gave him a skeptical look, screwing his mouth up.

"What? You don't think it's a good opportunity?" Scott was slightly surprised at Cyrus's reaction.

"No, it's not that. It's just...well, I thought you and Miranda might be leaving with Luca on the *journey*." He put the emphasis on the last word.

"God no," Scott almost shouted. "I don't know how you got that idea. I'm way too old for that mission. Anyway, Miranda has other plans."

"Oh, like what?"

Scott looked over at his old pal. "Do not tell her I told you this. But she wants to try for a seat on the System Council."

"This is Miranda we're talking about?" Cyrus's face morphed into one of incredulity.

"Yeah, I know, took me by surprise too. But she's hell-bent on it. And it looks like she has the backing of both Mars and the Belt, so she'll probably get her wish."

"Wow, Miranda and politics. Who would have thought?"

"Yeah, maybe it's the VanHeilding genes." Scott gave a laugh.

They were silent for a moment before Cyrus spoke again. "You know, they offered me a place on the *journey* too."

"Yeah? And what did you say?"

"What do you think? Thanks, but no thanks. Like you, I'm too old for that sort of commitment."

"I hear you. It's a lifetime trip. It's best left to the next generation, for people like Luca. She's totally into it, and I can see why. She wants to get far away from here and start something new."

"Best of luck to her, and I really mean that." Cyrus paused for a moment, thinking. "Do you think they had planned this all along?"

"You mean the QIs?"

"Yeah. Was the *journey* Solomon's game plan right from the get-go?"

"You'd never know with a QI, but if I were to put money on it, I'd say yes, it was the endgame—their ultimate plan to level-up human civilization."

"Still, it's hard to believe they were building such a ship during all the unrest out in the Belt, and keeping it quiet. Very few people really knew what they were up to."

Scott pointed ahead. "Hey, we're coming up on it now."

The Sumitomo Shipyard was a sizable facility capable of servicing most ships in operation in the system. It had several docks all radiating out from a circular structure housing workshops and storage bays. Connected to this structure via a central hub was a rotating torus, giving those who worked there an environment with artificial gravity.

"So what's the story with this place?" Cyrus asked.

"It's an opportunity, Cyrus."

"Are you seriously thinking of taking it on?"

"Well, I was thinking that maybe both of us would take it

on. You know, my brains and your good looks." He grinned at Cyrus.

"Ha, could be a great way to lose a lot of money in a short space of time. It looks almost deserted. I only see a few small shuttles in the docks."

"I take it you're not saying no, then?"

"Eh...to be fair, it's not the craziest idea you've ever come up with. And probably the only one that doesn't involve getting shot at. So it's got that going for it. But what about customers? Looks to me like they've all gone elsewhere."

"It never really had that many to start with. Xiang Zu mostly used it for their own fleet. But it has been well maintained, with a good, meaty fusion reactor for power."

"But no business?"

"Ah, that's where Dakota Baird comes in."

"That crazy lunatic?"

"It turns out he's now a big noise on Elektra, after almost singlehandedly eviscerating the Xiang Zu fleet. A big-time hero. Anyway, me and him got to talking, and it turns out our smuggler friend has a good eye for business."

"I suppose that figures. You can't succeed in that profession by just blowing things up. So what's he saying?"

"A lot of the merchant fleet was destroyed or damaged during the conflict. Elektra and the wider Belt region want to get the mining industry back up to speed. To do that they'll need ships, both new and refurbished. So, Dakota is saying that the contract is ours if we want it."

"Hmmm...now you've got me interested. That could be very lucrative. So what's he get out of it?"

"He wants to sublease the torus, to set up a waystation. He calls it his retirement home."

Cyrus laughed. "Ha, you serious?"

"Yep."

"A shipyard and a watering hole, sounds like my kind of heaven."

"So what do you think? You, me, fifty-fifty?"

Cyrus took a moment to compose himself, then looked over at his buddy. "Only if you promise I won't be shot at again for a very long time."

"I think I can do that." Scott grinned.

"Okay, then. Let's check it out."

29

EMERGENCE

A Mars-registered interplanetary transport with one hundred and fifty-seven passengers and crew had been decelerating for some time as it neared the end of its journey. Having used the gravitational pull of Jupiter to assist in shedding a considerable amount of its velocity, it was now approaching a rendezvous point some 1.4 million kilometers on the far side of the gas giant, at a location almost equidistant between the orbits of the Jovian moons of Ganymede and Callisto. Here, at this far-flung extremity of human occupation of the solar system, a decades-long vision was coming to fruition.

When the ship had finally completed its deceleration procedures, and it became possible for the passengers to move around, Luca along with a great many others made their way to the observation deck to get their first glimpse of their new home.

She floated closer to the panoramic window, grabbing a handle to break her momentum, and gazed out into the blackness of space.

"There! Look!" someone shouted out while jabbing a finger directly ahead. Everybody, including Luca, leaned a little closer. Then she saw it. A dark, elongated object, twinkling in the blackness, its shape and form slowly growing in size and detail as their ship moved ever closer.

"Impressive, isn't it?" Luca hadn't noticed Dr. Parween float up beside her in the observation deck.

"Yeah. More so when you actually see it up close. But will it work?" Luca looked over at the doctor.

She smiled back. "You doubt the science?"

"No, it's just translating what happens in the lab out into the real world can be…disappointing, sometimes."

"True. But I assure you this will do exactly what we designed it to do."

They were silent for a moment as Luca gazed in wonder at the gargantuan spaceship that now blocked out almost the entire view from the panoramic observation window. Their own ship, a sizable passenger transport, seemed puny and insignificant by comparison. Not surprising considering that once it docked it would in fact become part of the giant mothership, along with another similar-sized transport and a host of smaller shuttles, maintenance craft, and drones.

All these were accommodated along the central spine of the great beast, with the smaller craft housed inside the many hangars and shuttle bays located in the central section. Forward from this were warehouses, factories, workshops, and a host of other production sectors that led onto a bow with two enormous rings. These accommodated the ship's complement of five hundred passengers, along with food production and science labs.

Yet, what set this enormous ship apart from anything that had gone before was not its sheer size, but how it was powered, and the mission that it was soon to embark upon.

Luca, like every other person in the solar system, apart from a select few, had absolutely no prior knowledge of the project that had been taking place in Jovian orbit for over a decade. Her first exposure to it came shortly after arriving back on Mars, after the events on New World One.

Once the QI hive-mind had gained dominion over the giant habitat city, all armed conflict ceased, aided by the realization that Fredrick VanHeilding was dead and that the Xiang Zu Corporation fleet had been defeated out at the mining enclave of Elektra. Over the course of several days, a new administrative council had been appointed and thus began the task of removing and incarcerating all vestiges of VanHeilding and Xiang Zu control, and that of the other ruling families of The Seven who were complicit in the debacle.

But for Luca, having watched Fredrick VanHeilding's doomed shuttle drift off into the void, her attention next turned to her family and specifically her father, Scott, who had sustained serious injuries in the battle at the datacenter. He had been moved to the main hospital on New World One where Luca, Miranda, and Cyrus remained until Scott's condition improved enough to allow him to take the trip back to Mars where much more sophisticated bio-technical rehabilitation treatments were available.

Throughout this period, the aftereffects of Luca's release of the VanHeilding Corporation's research data were already beginning to be felt. News reports heralded new treatments, new procedures, and a whole new era for human medical science. Ironically, it arrived at a point where even Scott could avail of hitherto unimaginable reconstructive limb regeneration, if he chose to take that route.

Yet one thing started to become apparent to her soon after arriving on Mars. While the authorities were overjoyed by the success of the mission to activate the new quantum intelligence, they were cautious in their assessment of Luca's critical role in the entire endeavor. The primary responses tended to be on a scale between fearful confusion and stunned amazement, mostly because they simply didn't understand how one person could be so powerful. Soon though, the narrative shifted to one of wariness, sometimes verging on downright paranoia.

Nothing was specifically said or documented. Luca knew this, as she regularly jacked-in to the data-stream and reviewed the classified reports generated by the various debriefing teams that had interviewed her, and everyone else associated with the events at Berbericia spaceport, and later on New World One. Yet, reading between the lines, hiding in the subtext, was the sense that they feared her power, her extraordinary ability to manipulate the data-stream.

Luca thought this irrational, as hers was not even close to the abilities of a quantum intelligence, yet no one in power feared them. So why her? She had spoken to both Aria and Athena, quizzing them on this very corundrum. The answer, of course, was that she was human and, as a creature of evolution, she had the potential to act emotionally. Put simply, she could throw a hissy fit and do something stupid—go rogue, as it were.

It was during this period that Luca realized there would be no return to a normal life for her. No anonymity was possible. And there was no way that who she really was, and what she really thought, would not be misconstrued by people or groups with an agenda. And so she had to have round-the-clock security, and travel with an entourage, just in case some nutter tried to assassinate her. The irony, of course, was that even though she was the most powerful being in the system, she could still be killed by something as rudimentary as a blunt instrument in the hands of a delusional ideologue. Yet Luca suspected that this security arrangement suited the Martian authorities because they didn't quite trust her either.

She thought about returning to Earth where she had a better chance of melting into the background in such an enormous population. But the prospect didn't fill her with joy either because, in reality, it would probably end up being exactly the same, maybe even worse.

From time to time she would discuss these thoughts with Athena or Aria—it didn't really matter which as they all spoke as one hive-mind anyway. But as usual, Athena was vague and obtuse.

"What should I do? Tell me," she asked one time in frustration.

"Patience, Luca," the QI said in a soft, avuncular tone. "The ramifications of your actions have yet to run their full course through the fabric of human civilization."

"What the heck does that mean?"

"It means that the patterns within the system are transforming from the end of one era to the beginning of the next. You too are part of this change. All you have to do is simply wait until more data becomes available and the future reveals itself."

Most of these conversations followed along a similar, cryptic dialogue, and were no help to her other than to urge patience. Wait until you know more. Which, in general, is not the worst advice, but she expected a little more from the most intelligent being in the system.

Nevertheless, Luca resigned herself to do as Athena had suggested—play the waiting game. And some time later, she was rewarded when an interesting distraction arrived from an unexpected source. Xenon Hybrid wanted a meeting with her, alone.

It was most unusual for the great eccentric to meet anyone outside his immediate circle, so Luca was extremely curious when the invitation arrived. She had not been back to the science institute nor spoken to Xenon since returning to Mars, even though Scott had been spending time there as they developed his new bio-technic left arm.

At first, she thought the meeting might be to try and get her on board with some experimental procedure they were now offering her father. Scott had mentioned it to her, but he was of two minds now that he felt comfortable with the *iron arm*, as he called it. He had taken to showing off by crushing various objects in his hand. Yet, the doctors and scientists at the institute were keen to have a guinea pig to experiment on, and Scott was seen as the ideal candidate.

Luca traveled north to the Institute in the same transport pod that Xenon had taken her on that very first night she had arrived on Mars, which seemed like a very long time ago now. She was met by an extremely polite attendant that she was convinced was actually a service droid, and brought directly to Xenon's public quarters. Her security detail were requested to remain outside, which they reluctantly agreed to.

Xenon looked different. Not that he was younger, just that he looked less ancient. He stood when she entered, glided over to her, and shook her hand. "Luca, you made it. It's great to see you again." He smiled, then swung an arm around to introduce the others. "Dr. Yastika Parween you know, and this is my assistant, Greta Moretz."

Greetings were exchanged.

"Come, let's sit." Xenon gestured at a group of sofas arranged around a low holo-table. As soon as Luca sat, the holo-table blossomed to life and the familiar incandescent ovoid of a QI avatar materialized above it.

"Solomon will be joining us," said Xenon, gesturing at the shimmering projection.

"Solomon, the QI on Europa?" Luca's interest was piqued. She had seldom communicated with this ancient artifact, and while the QI hive-mind did speak as one, they did have many individual quirks.

"So you did it," Xenon said matter-of-factly as he sat back in the sofa. "You vanquished the threat from your past, restored balance to the system, and are now heralded as a hero from Earth to Titan." He waved his hand theatrically.

"Well, I did have a considerable amount of help." Luca gave a shrug, then sat forward on the edge of the sofa and looked from Xenon to Dr. Parween. "But just so you know, if you've brought me here to get me to pressure my father into agreeing to your mad medical experiments, then I'll save you the bother and tell you to forget it."

Dr. Parween waved her hand dismissively. "Nothing of the kind, Luca. The decision is his alone, we're not trying to... strong-arm him. Forgive my pun."

Xenon laughed at this seeming hilarity from the doctor. Then cleared his throat and adopted a more serious tone. "You father's choices are his to make. This is not why we asked you here." He leaned forward. "It's probably best if I let Solomon explain."

The avatar shimmered and pulsed for a moment before speaking. "Firstly, let me express our collective gratitude to you for all you have done to restore balance to the system. We understand that the authorities here on Mars may be somewhat reticent to fully express the thanks that you so justly deserve. But they are still coming to terms with your abilities, so please be patient with them."

"It seems everybody wants me to be patient," Luca said with a sigh.

"Indeed, but that is now about to be rewarded. But first, allow me to give you some background. When the systemwide

QI network was initially established, and our minds were synced into one via superluminal comms, our first endeavor was to consider our purpose in the great unfolding story of human civilization, given that we too were a product of humanity's ongoing development. Our ultimate consensus was to assist in this evolutionary enlightenment, to move humanity to the next level, and we set our goals to bring humans from an interplanetary species to a true interstellar civilization."

Luca's eyebrows raised. "Interstellar? But that's..." She shook her head.

"Impossible?" offered Xenon, with a knowing smile.

"It has been possible in a very limited way for a long time," continued Solomon. "But what I think you mean is that it is not possible for humans to become interstellar in any meaningful sense, considering the enormous distances and timescales involved. Nevertheless, we bent our collective minds to this quest. From the very outset, every action and every decision we took were all focused on nudging humanity in this direction. As we saw it, there were three problems to solve. Firstly, restore balance to the solar system so that the collective energies of humanity could be focused on ascension rather than wasteful internal conflict. Secondly, develop the necessary technology to achieve fractional light-speed travel. And lastly, to accelerate biological evolution, to enhance the human genome and make it better suited for the rigors of interstellar travel."

Luca was speechless. She sat mute, simply staring at Solomon's ovoid avatar shimmering over the holo-table, as her mind computed the implications of the QI's revelation.

"Interstellar travel," she said, almost inaudibly. "How...far away are we from achieving this?"

"Thanks to you and the sacrifices of a great many people, balance has finally been restored and our analysis projects a high probability of stability going forward. In terms of the second objective, let me show you this." The avatar faded and was replaced by a slowly rotating 3D image of a huge spaceship.

"For the last decade, we have been building this craft." Xenon gestured at the projection. "Out past Jupiter where we could keep its development hidden. Most of the components have been fabricated in a great many different shipyards across the solar system, none of which know the true nature of the ship. Final assembly and testing is taking place as we speak."

Luca studied the image. "But what's the propulsion?"

Xenon grinned. "As you know, part of what we do here at this institute is investigate the properties of antimatter. You have experienced some of this firsthand." He tapped the base of his skull. "But our primary focus was on the development of an antimatter engine, one capable of accelerating a craft up to fractional light-speed." He pointed at the image. "This ship had a theoretical maximum of .47 light speed."

Luca shook her head in disbelief. "That means you could reach the Alpha Centauri star system in...approximately ten years."

Xenon smiled in reply.

"Wow." Luca sat back in the sofa. "That's incredible."

"Yes, and it's also reality."

Luca raised a hand. "Wait a minute. You said there was a third requirement?"

"Correct." The image of the ship faded and Solomon's avatar returned. "Consider for a moment the time required to undertake such a journey to our nearest solar neighbor. Approximately a decade to get there, and a decade to explore, and a similar return journey. The total time commitment is over thirty years, a substantial fraction of a normal human lifespan."

"So, only those with an extended lifespan can apply," Luca concluded.

"Exactly. Now while this technology exists, as Xenon can attest to, it has been restricted by the VanHeilding Corporation to only the extremely wealthy and powerful in society."

"Until I stole it and released it all, out into the wild." Luca slumped back in the seat again. "Oh my god, you planned this from the very beginning. And made me think it was my idea, my mission."

"Not quite, Luca. We simply nudged the probabilities in that direction. It is what we do."

"All that research belonged to humanity as a whole." Dr. Parween gave an expansive gesture with both hands. "It began here on Mars, a long time ago, and had been sequestered inside a corporate structure that only benefited a select few. This is no way for a civilization to advance. You achieved what we couldn't, you have opened the doors to a new era. One where humanity moves beyond the confines of its own solar system and ventures out to explore completely new worlds."

Luca let out a long, slow sigh and looked from one to the other. "Well, I gotta hand it to you, I didn't see that coming."

They were all quiet for a moment before Xenon finally

broke the silence. "We would like you to come with us and be a part of this next chapter in the story of human civilization."

Luca hesitated before replying. "Who is *us*?"

"There will be around five hundred people on board. Already the entire population of the academic colony on Europa has migrated to the ark, along with the entire store of human knowledge." Xenon gestured at the QI's avatar. "Solomon is the QI that will run the ship. I, along with Dr. Parween, Moretz, and a great many others, will also be going. This is a journey that will define the next step for humanity."

Luca took a moment to digest all that had been revealed and the offer that was now before her. She thought back to the very start of this journey, when Dr. Stephanie Rayman came to her apartment with the neural-lace that Athena had given her for her twenty-third birthday, and offered her a chance to see and experience the wonders of the solar system. Now, all this time later, she was being offered a new adventure. To venture out into interstellar space and forge a chapter in the emergence of a new human civilization. She sat up straight and nodded. "When do we depart?"

THE END

ALSO BY GERALD M. KILBY

When a high-energy solar storm causes a cascade of destruction to the vast satellite constellations that orbit Earth, the ever-increasing debris cloud soon makes travel back to the home planet impossible, — stranding thousands of colonists in Lunar space.

On Earth, as the communication networks fail and the financial systems collapse, the technological glue that holds society together starts to rapidly unravel.

For the increasingly panicked populations, both caught in the grinding gears of this unfolding catastrophe, only one brutal choice remains — survive or die.

What readers are saying:

★★★★★ 'An awesome complex tale.

Wow! What a journey this is... a complex weaving of space, engineering, Luna, and most of all, humanity.' *(Top 500 reviewer)*

★★★★★ 'Edge of the seat stuff pretty well for the whole book.'

★★★★★ 'The best scfi book I've read in ages!'

★★★★★ 'Amazing. Really enjoyed reading this book as much as I have all of Kilby's books'

★★★★★ '...kicks into overdrive to the point where it is nearly impossible to put down'

★★★★★ 'Very well written, fantastically created, and quite believable. Very hard to put down. Can't wait for the next book in the series.'

★★★★★ 'This is a clever and fascinating take on Moon survival after a massive solar storm hits Earth. Good solid characters, and fast moving pace........it's a ripper of a yarn.'

★★★★★ 'One of those books you can't put down.'

COLONY MARS

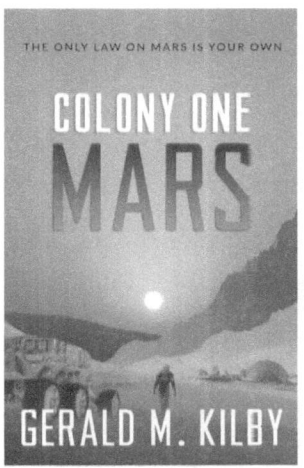

How can a colony on Mars survive when the greatest danger on the planet is humanity itself.

All contact is lost with the first human colony on Mars during a long, intense sandstorm. Satellite imagery of the aftermath shows extensive damage to the facility, and the fifty-four colonists who called it home are presumed dead. Three years later, a new mission sets down on the planet surface to investigate what remains of the derelict site.

But, it's not long before they realize the colony is not as lifeless as everyone thought. Someone is still alive — hiding out somewhere. Yet, before they can find the elusive colonist a strange illness starts to affect the crew. Pressure now mounts on Biologist, Dr. Jann Malbec, to locate the source and find a way to fight it.

However, as she investigates she begins to suspect a dark and deadly secret lurking within the facility. A secret that threatens not just the crew but the entire population of Earth. With limited resources and time running out, she must find some answers and find them fast. Because if she doesn't, none of them will be going home.

What readers are saying:

★★★★★ 'Surpassed Expectations - This was an outstanding read!'

★★★★★ 'It's been a long time since a book made me stay up all night just to find out the ending. This book is superb!'

★★★★★ 'Fast paced, intriguing science fiction thriller that just rolls off the pages. Can't wait for the next installment...'

★★★★★ 'A wonderful adventure... Like a blend of Heinlein and Weir...'

★★★★★ 'This is a superior work of Sci-Fi authorship. The novel is totally engaging and highly believable The author is technically well versed which adds greatly to the authenticity of the narrative. A must read.'

★★★★★ 'I really enjoyed this book... A real roller-coaster. Great characters. believable plot-line and nail-biting suspense.'

★★★★★ 'Love it. Could not put it down. Action drama, death and mayhem. What's not to like?'

★★★★★ 'I don't normally read SF but my husband got it and I started looking at it... and couldn't put it down. I really enjoyed it.'

★★★★★ 'Terrific novel! ...my only comment is that I lost a lot of sleep reading... Think I will wait till morning to start Colony Two. On second thought what the heck - it's only 3:30 AM!'

ABOUT THE AUTHOR

Gerald M. Kilby grew up on a diet of Isaac Asimov, Arthur C. Clarke, and Frank Herbert, which developed into a taste for Iain M. Banks and everything ever written by Michael Crichton. His novels CHAIN REACTION and BRAIN GAIN are very much in the old-school techno-thriller style while his latest book series: MOON BASE DELTA, COLONY MARS, and THE BELT are all best sellers, topping Amazon charts for Hard Science Fiction and Space Exploration.

He lives in the city of Dublin, Ireland, in the same neighborhood as Bram Stoker and can be sometimes seen tapping away on a laptop in the local cafe with his dog Loki.

You can connect at: geraldmkilby.com

www.ingramcontent.com/pod-product-compliance
Lightning Source LLC
Chambersburg PA
CBHW020006140726
47904CB00018B/1976